Chase knocked on the door.

Nothing.

Exchanging a glance with Caitlin, he pounded with a fist. "Willie? Hey, Willie, are you in there?"

Not a sound from inside. Concern flooded Caitlin's features. "Maybe he's ill and can't come to the door. I think you should go in, Chase. He might need help."

She was right. Chase pounded on the door once again. "Willie, I'm coming in."

He unlocked the door, stepped inside. And froze.

Willie lay facedown on a large throw rug, his head at an unnatural sideways angle. An incredible amount of blood soaked the thin rug. Chase's stomach lurched. From his vantage point, he could see that Willie's throat had been cut.

Just like the man in the park. Just like Kevin.

Chase backed out and pulled the door closed.

"Chase?" Caitlin sounded worried. "Is everything okay?"

Chase swallowed hard. "We'd better call 9-1-1. Willie's dead."

Books by Virginia Smith

Love Inspired Suspense

Murder by Mushroom
Bluegrass Peril
A Taste of Murder
Murder at Eagle Summit
Scent of Murder

VIRGINIA SMITH

A lifelong lover of books, Virginia Smith has always enjoyed immersing herself in fiction. In her mid-twenties she wrote her first story and discovered that writing well is harder than it looks; it took many years to produce a book worthy of publication. During the daylight hours she steadily climbed the corporate ladder and stole time to write late at night after the kids were in bed. With the publication of her first novel, she left her twenty-year corporate profession to devote her energy to her passion—writing stories that honor God and bring a smile to the faces of her readers. When she isn't writing, Ginny and her husband, Ted, enjoy exploring the extremes of nature—snow skiing in the mountains of Utah, motorcycle riding on the curvy roads of central Kentucky and scuba diving in the warm waters of the Caribbean. Visit www.VirginiaSmith.org.

VIRGINIA SMITH
SCENT *of* MURDER

Steeple
Hill®

Published by Steeple Hill Books™

STEEPLE HILL BOOKS

Steeple
Hill®

Recycling programs
for this product may
not exist in your area.

ISBN-13: 978-0-373-44343-7

SCENT OF MURDER

www.SteepleHill.com

Printed in U.S.A.

Blessed are the merciful,
for they will be shown mercy.
—*Matthew* 5:7

I'm grateful to many people who helped me take this story from idea to published book.

Thanks to

My husband, Ted, for helping me work out the details and for shopping with me in Little Nashville, though that's probably his least favorite thing to do in the world.

A terrific group of friends with whom Ted and I have spent many delightful hours in Brown County: Trudy Kirk (my shopping buddy and retail therapist), Bob Young, and two we'll see again on the other side, Larry Kirk and Paul Morris.

Janet Stephens from Candle Makers on the Square in Bowling Green, Kentucky, for openly sharing her knowledge and helping me understand the candle-making process. And Shawn Freeman, L.A.P.D.

The CWFI Critique Group for brainstorming all sorts of crazy things that can be stored in candles: Tracy Ruckman, Sherry Kyle, Vicki Tiede, Amy Barkman, Amy Smith, Ann Knowles and Richard Leonard. And special thanks to Tracy for reading this manuscript in its roughest form and offering excellent suggestions.

My agent, Wendy Lawton, for encouragement above and beyond the call of duty.

All the people at Steeple Hill Books who continually give to me freely of their time and expertise, especially Elizabeth Mazer, Tina Colombo, Louise Rozett and Krista Stroever.

And finally, eternal thanks to my Lord Jesus, without whom nothing would matter.

ONE

The rising sun glimmered in the eastern sky as Chase Hollister followed a well-defined trail that skirted the edge of Brown County State Park. He maintained a brisk pace, though low branches from the dense trees made running impossible. Night clung to the forest around him with stubborn determination, even as tendrils of sunlight threatened its tenacious hold. Chase welcomed the shadowy darkness. It suited his mood.

A lingering chill penetrated his T-shirt and sent a shiver rippling through his body. Nights in early May here in Indiana were still pretty cold. He should have grabbed a lightweight jacket on his way out of the house.

Scratch that. He should have kept to the open road for his morning run, where the heat of exertion would have kept him warm. What possessed him to come to the park before dawn—again?

Chase climbed over a dead tree limb lying across the path. No matter how determined he was not to haunt this place, he kept returning.

Not as often as before. A year ago, right after the tragedy—his mind skipped across the details, best not go there—he'd wandered these trails almost daily. His parents assumed he'd found some sort of comfort in surrounding himself with nature. Maybe they thought he was praying. And Chase had done some praying, if his repeated questions of *Why, Lord? Why didn't I see it? How could I miss it?* counted as prayers. But no answers had been forthcoming, and the questions still tortured Chase, almost a year later.

And he still wandered the park trails every few weeks. How sad was that?

The shadows lost their tenuous grip on the wooded area around him, and Chase could now make out a few more details. A movement up ahead turned out to be a deer. He caught sight of a patch of white fur as it scurried off and disappeared into the forest, no doubt startled to see anyone out at this early hour. Something rustled the thick green leaves in the tree overhead. The residents of the park were waking.

He heard the stream before he saw it, smelled the fresh, rich scent of mud from the shore. The trail turned sharply and ran alongside the wide stream for fifty yards or so, to the place where the path ended at the road. Chase tensed when he glimpsed a dark structure, the covered bridge that stood sentinel over the north entrance to the park. And beneath it…

He set his teeth together. The place that drew him here. That haunted him.

How many times had he told himself he would not come back here, that he needed to put the past behind him and move on? And yet, here he was.

His step slowed as he neared the trail's end. The stream splashed along beside him, the sound an almost joyful counterpoint to his dire thoughts. *I was too focused on myself, on my stupid infatuation with Leslie. If I'd paid more attention to my friend, surely I would have known. I could have helped him.*

His throat tightened like a clenched fist, a familiar feeling lately. *I'm so sorry, Kevin.*

The sun had not yet risen above the trees to his left, so the wide, muddy area beneath the bridge was still in shadows. Try though he might, Chase couldn't stop himself from staring at the place where the nightmare had begun.

His footsteps faltered. The shore wasn't empty. Something was there, something big. Black. It was…

Chase's mouth went dry. A car. The front tires rested in the water, the rear end angled upward on the steep bank.

He broke into a run. One corner of his mind noted the angle of the tire tracks in the soft soil as he splashed into the stream. The car had been driven, or maybe pushed, off the two-lane road a few feet before entering the covered bridge. Icy water wet Chase's sweatpants up to the knees. He barely noticed. His fingers grasped the door handle and jerked. Locked. He shielded his eyes and peered through the window.

Acid surged into Chase's throat. He jerked away, stomach roiling. No doubt at all what had killed the person inside. Dark stains covered the man's clothing and the car's interior. An ugly wound gaped in his throat.

Just like Kevin.

Chase stumbled to the shore and fell to his knees. Mud seeped through his pants, but he didn't move.

Lord, no—it can't happen again.

"I'm really sorry, Caitlin. I just can't take the time off work right now."

Sincerity filled the voice on the phone, but Caitlin Saylor couldn't quite bring herself to accept Jazzy's apology. They'd planned this trip for two months, and Caitlin had been looking forward to the five-day vacation with her musical-trio friends more than she cared to admit. But both Liz and Jazzy had cancelled last week.

Correction. Not cancelled. They'd abandoned her. That's what it felt like.

Stop it. They can't help it if they don't have enough vacation time.

Of course, the reason Liz and Jazzy had used up all their vacation time was the root of Caitlin's hurt feelings. Over the past couple of years they had played their classical music at dozens of weddings. Now the trio was breaking up because Jazzy and Liz were both getting married themselves, and moving away. And Caitlin wasn't.

Abandoned, in more ways than one.

She switched the cordless phone to her left hand, leaving her right free to rinse her coffee mug and set it in the top rack of the dishwasher. "You *are* still planning to take off Friday afternoon and get up there in time for the rehearsal, aren't you? We have a commitment to the bride. I can't play an entire wedding and a reception as a flute solo."

"You know we wouldn't duck out on our last performance. Liz and I are both leaving work at noon. We'll meet you in Indiana at three. That'll give us plenty of time to get to the rehearsal by four."

They're not leaving much room for error. What if they have car trouble or something? Caitlin was glad her friend couldn't see her scowl. She didn't want to be accused of acting childish—even though she was.

"The Internet says there are hundreds of craft shops and art galleries in that little town. You've got two and a half days to search out the best shopping spots," Jazzy went on. "We'll have Friday night after the rehearsal, and most of the day Saturday, since the wedding isn't until evening. So, take a notepad and make a list, okay? And if you find something really good, buy it for me as a wedding present."

Caitlin picked up the dishrag and gave the counter a final, savage swipe. That was *exactly* what she wanted to do for the next few days—shop alone. *Not!*

But she told Jazzy, "I will." Did her voice sound as forlorn as she felt?

"Listen, are you sure you want to go up there by yourself? Why don't you call the hotel and tell them we've been delayed and we'll be checking in two days later?"

She glanced across the dinette area, at the luggage sitting next to the front door of her apartment. Sassy, her Lhasa Apso, kept running over to sniff it.

"I'm sure." She forced a confidence she didn't feel into her tone.

"Well, make sure your cell phone is fully charged. Do you have mace in your purse?"

Caitlin paused. "Why would I need mace?"

"What if you have a flat tire and you're stranded on the side of the road when some sicko stops? You need protection."

"You are such an alarmist, Jazzy. No, I don't have mace, but I do have my trusty pocket knife."

"Like that little Girl Scout toy could stop anybody."

Caitlin heaved an exaggerated sigh. "I won't need to stop anyone. My tires are fine. But if anything does happen, I'm perfectly capable of changing a tire. Don't worry about me. I can take care of myself."

"If you say so." Jazzy sounded hesitant. "Call me when you get there, and let me know how the hotel room is. You've got Lysol, right?"

That drew a grudging laugh out of Caitlin. Compulsively clean Jazzy never went anywhere without a plentiful supply of antibacterial cleaning products. "I'll call you. Good-bye, Jazzy."

Caitlin replaced the phone in its cradle on the kitchen wall. Melancholy feelings returned as she glanced around the too-clean kitchen. She'd spent so much time cleaning lately, she could be accused of having germaphobic tendencies herself. But what else did she have to fill her evenings?

Sassy charged into the room and hopped on her hind legs, yapping. *At least someone still wants to spend time with me.* Caitlin scooped Sassy into her arms and buried her face in the dog's neck. If a few tears fell into the fuzzy fur, well, it wasn't the first time.

She carried Sassy into the living room, where her suitcase, flute, and music portfolio stood ready to be loaded into the car. Maybe she ought to do as Jazzy suggested. If she postponed until Friday, she could make the trip with her friends.

But she'd been looking forward to this minivacation for months. Her schedule was clear. She'd told all her students there would be no lessons for the remainder of the week. The deposit had been paid for Sassy to spend five days at Raintree Pet Resort. True, they'd probably let her cancel the first couple of days if she decided to stay home.

But why should she? So she could sit around and feel sorry for herself? She clenched her teeth. *Stop it, Caitlin!* Her friends' upcoming weddings were ruining her mood lately. Not that she wasn't thrilled for Jazzy and Liz, but *both* of them planning weddings at the same time? That's all they talked about anymore. If she waited to drive up with them, no doubt the entire three-hour trip to Indiana would be full of wedding talk and plans for happy homemaking. They seemed to forget that while they were busy planning for their new lives, she was being left out in the cold.

Or maybe they just don't care.

Caitlin thrust the thought away. Of course her friends cared about her. She was just feeling sorry for herself. After all, it hadn't been so long since she was the only one of the three who even had a steady boyfriend. Oh, how the tables could turn in the span of a single year. Now Jazzy and Liz were both getting married, and she was facing life as an old maid.

The familiar ache in her chest turned to anger and threatened to send more tears into her eyes. If Glenn were here right now she'd…she'd…she'd kick him in the shin, that's what she'd do. Serve him right, after leading her on for three years and then dumping her for someone else. *I wasted the best years of my life.* The thought only made her angrier. He'd reduced her to thinking in clichés!

Sassy wriggled around in her arms to lick her face. The attempt to calm her brought a smile to Caitlin's lips.

"I've got to get on with life," she told the dog. "I'm driving up to Nashville, Indiana, by myself, and I'm going to make myself have a good time. It'll be like a retreat. I'll take my bible and spend some serious time in prayer. That'll give me a new perspective for sure."

She gave Sassy a final snuggle, then set her on the floor. Standing around here was getting her nowhere. Time to get a move on. In more ways than one.

TWO

Chase leaned against a tree, his face angled away from the activity around the car. The sick knot that had formed in his stomach since the moment he saw the vehicle halfway in the stream refused to let up. Instead, it tightened every time he glanced that way.

The police had closed down this section of the park by stringing yellow tape across the road up above, fifty feet beyond the bridge. He kept his face turned away from that area, too. He'd caught a glimpse of television cameras there, and the last thing he wanted was to be identified on the news as the person who discovered the body of a dead guy. Only a matter of time before some reporter recognized the similarities to last year's crime, and a little digging would reveal Chase's involvement with that one, remote though it had been.

The police had certainly already made the connection. He'd given his statement, told them everything he could, but had been informed that he could not leave yet. They were holding him here until he could be questioned by—

The sound of footsteps crunching dead leaves behind him interrupted his thoughts. Chase half turned and caught sight of the approaching plainclothes policeman. His spine stiff-

ened. As he expected, the man who approached was familiar.
And unwelcome.

Detective Jenkins.

Jenkins's gaze locked on Chase as though daring him to
turn away. Chase stood his ground and returned the hard stare
without flinching.

"Hollister." The detective's head dipped in a nod, but his
eyes did not release Chase's. "Been a while."

"Yes, it has." Chase was proud that his voice betrayed none
of the turmoil he felt. He'd been interrogated last year by
Jenkins. Not an experience he cared to repeat, but given the
circumstances, he couldn't see any way to avoid talking with
the guy. Chase squared his shoulders. "I guess you want to
hear how I found the body."

Jenkins didn't answer immediately. In his left hand he
clutched a rolled-up sheet of paper, which he tapped on his
thigh. His right hand rose to tug a lock of hair behind his ear.
Sunlight reflected off a few strands of silver mixed in with the
brown that Chase didn't remember from last year.

Finally, Jenkins gave a slow nod. "Eventually. First, I want
to know why you happened to be in the park, at *this* particular spot—" he gestured vaguely toward the car beneath the
bridge "—so early in the morning."

Chase scuffed the toe of his running shoe in the grass. "I
run a few miles every morning before work."

Jenkins cocked his head. "Don't you live pretty far from
here? Out past that factory your family owns?"

"I drove. No doubt your deputies have already found my
car in the parking lot a few miles back."

The detective's eyes narrowed. "This is a mighty strange
place for a morning run. I'd think you, of all people, would
stay as far away from here as possible."

Chase didn't reply. What could he say? Jenkins was right.

Returning to the place where his best friend had been killed wasn't just strange. It was downright weird.

After an uncomfortable silence, Jenkins unrolled the paper and scanned it. "I have your statement here. Says you left your house at five this morning, drove to the park, walked from there to here, where you spotted the victim's vehicle. You tried to open the door, but it was locked. So you backtracked to your car to get your cell phone and called 911." He raised his eyes from the paper without moving his head. "That right?"

"Yes, except I didn't backtrack across the trail. I went up on the road and ran to the parking lot because it was faster."

"Did you get a look at the body?"

Chase closed his eyes. If only he hadn't. He nodded.

"Recognize him?"

"I—" Chase swallowed. "I don't think so. I couldn't see him very well. I mainly saw a lot of blood."

The image had been burned in his mind's eye. Kevin's family had chosen cremation, so Chase's last memory of his friend was of him waving good-bye as he left the factory after a long day's work. Only now, Chase's active imagination put Kevin's face on that body in the car, the one with the gaping wound in the throat. He doubted he'd ever be able to forget it.

"There's a lot of blood when a body bleeds out."

The detective was studying him with an intensity that Chase remembered from last year. He didn't like it then, either.

"Listen, I'm late for work. Is there anything else you need me for here?"

Jenkins paused. Then he rolled the paper once again into a tube and tapped it against his palm. "Not at the moment. But I'm sure I'm going to have more questions." His stare grew hard. "You're not planning to leave town anytime soon, are you?"

Chase's mouth went dry for the second time that morning. Was he a suspect?

He probably was. Even he had to admit it looked odd for the best friend of one murder victim to find the body of a second victim in the exact same place, murdered in the exact same way. He was lucky Jenkins wasn't hauling him in and charging him with murder.

Wordlessly, Chase shook his head.

"All right, then you can go." The detective started to turn away, then stopped. "I'll be in touch."

The words sounded like a threat.

Ed dug at his eyes with a thumb and forefinger as he stumbled toward the coffeepot. His wife sat at the kitchen table reading the newspaper.

"Why didn't you wake me up?" he snapped. "I'm going to be late again."

She didn't raise her eyes from her perusal of the paper. "I tried. Three times. Getting you up in the morning after you've been out drinking is more like a resurrection than an awakening." She turned a page. "Besides, it's not like anybody there's watching a clock."

Ed bit back a sharp response as he snatched a cup off the mug tree on the counter and sloshed coffee into it. Better to hold his tongue than to argue with Janie this morning. She'd probably heard him come home last night, though he'd tried to be quiet. But when he'd tripped over the doorjamb and knocked into the hall table, the crash had been loud enough to wake her up. At least she didn't flip on the light and yell at him when he got into bed, like she did last time. He hadn't meant to get rough with her, but she ought to know better than to nag him when he'd had a snootful.

The house was quiet. Too quiet. It emphasized the pounding ache in his head. He spoke just to break the silence. "Kids left for school?"

Most mornings, Janie chattered like a monkey. She must be mad at him. He could just see the top of her silver-streaked dark head nod behind the open newspaper.

Ed snatched the remote control off the table and pointed in the direction of the small television they kept on the kitchen counter. The pair who anchored the local morning news show appeared. Bright red letters scrolling across the bottom proclaimed, *Breaking News!* Ed punched up the volume.

"…to report the discovery of a body inside a car at the bottom of a steep embankment near the park's north entrance. Medics arrived shortly after and declared the man dead. The police have not yet issued a statement, so the victim has not been identified. Stay tuned to Channel 13 for the latest updates on this disturbing situation."

Coffee sloshed onto the counter as Ed slammed his mug down. He punched the off button as a curse escaped his lips. The remote control missed the table and hit the floor. The back popped off and batteries rolled across the kitchen.

"Hey, you broke it." Janie gave him a narrow-eyed look over the top of the paper. "What's the matter with you?"

Ed ignored her. He slammed out the back door toward his car.

That idiot! He should have known better than to leave the job in the hands of a two-bit moron. Ed could have handled the guy himself, roughed him up a little. He would have listened to reason. No need for someone else to die.

You just couldn't trust anyone in this business.

By the time Chase arrived at the family candle factory for work, the news had broken—another murder victim discovered at Brown County State Park. He'd called his parents on the way home to grab a shower, not only to let them know what was going on, but to explain why he would be late for work.

Mom had been understandably upset, but promised not to mention anything to their employees. Dad, who had taken over the cooking duties when he'd retired a year ago, responded with his usual brand of comfort. "Sorry, son. Drop by tonight and I'll toss something on the grill."

Now that Chase was finally at work, he was determined to keep a low profile and get some paperwork done. But it seemed everyone wanted to talk about the day's hottest news. He considered closing the office door so he wasn't such an easy target, but he knew the open-door policy was interpreted literally by the employees at Good Things in Wax. Closed doors made people nervous.

The scent of the previous afternoon's pour lingered heavily in the air. Naturally it had to be Cinnamon Red Hots. The strong smell always made his eyes burn. He didn't need to walk around with red eyes—especially not today.

"Did you hear the news, Chase?" Irene Bledsoe stood in the doorway and clutched the straps on her insulated lunch bag with both hands. Apparently the police had not identified him to the reporters, thank goodness.

"I heard." Seated behind one of the two desks in the crowded office, Chase offered the woman a polite smile. She'd been one of the first employees Grandpa Samson had hired back in the seventies when he expanded the family business.

"I wonder if it's related to…" She licked her pale lips nervously. "Uh, you know."

Oh, yeah. He knew. But he didn't want to talk about it, certainly not with one of his employees, no matter how long she'd been employed by his family.

Irene lowered her voice to a near whisper. "Maybe the police will get some leads from this case that will help them with the first one. I never believed that story the paper printed. Kevin Duncan was a good boy, no matter what they said."

Chase managed a nod. Irene was right. Nobody knew that better than him. Without a word, Chase went back to his paperwork. After staring a moment, the woman headed for the back.

He hadn't written three numbers on his inventory report before Alex Young stepped into the spot Irene had vacated. "You hear about the body they found over at the park this morning?"

Chase nodded but didn't look up.

"The radio said the guy's throat was cut."

Chase copied another item number onto his ledger. "I heard that."

"Kinda spooky, don't you think? That's the second one. Somebody down at the Dairy Dip said they found this guy around the same place, too."

Chase raised his head slowly and met Alex's gaze. He kept his expression carefully blank.

Alex took a backward step. "I'll just get on in there and see about the next pour."

"Good idea."

Chase returned to his report. Not two minutes later, his cousin, Korey, breezed into the office and threw himself in the chair behind the second desk.

"Seen the television lately? They found another body in the park this morning. Sca-ry. I hope this doesn't end up hurting business."

Teeth clenched to hold back a resigned sigh, Chase tossed his pencil on the ledger. He might be able to avoid discussing the day's hottest news with the factory employees, but his cousin was a different matter. Subtle hints were lost on Korey.

"What do you mean? How can this hurt business?"

"You know. Tourists." Korey used his forefingers as drumsticks on the edge of the desk. "If tourists find out two people have had their throats slit in these parts, they're probably not going to want to come to the area. They won't be shopping, which means the candle shops won't be placing any new orders, which means we won't be making any sales." He ended his drum solo with a flourish and grinned. "I thought you, being a college boy and all, would have figured that out all by yourself."

He had to admire Korey's logic, even if it was flawed. More proof of a fact he'd long known—his hyperactive cousin may not have the patience and temperament for school, but he sure had a knack for business. His instincts were some of the best Chase had ever seen, and sometimes that counted for more than education.

"I don't think we have anything to worry about. If word gets out, people might avoid the state park, but they're not going to stop coming to Little Nashville. Besides, Internet sales are climbing. If you'd take a look at that P&L statement I gave you last week—"

"Ah, you know I don't have time for that. You're the one who's good at number crunching. I'd rather spend my time getting my hands dirty." Korey jumped out of the chair and headed for the door. Nothing held the guy in place for very long.

"You don't fool me, bucko." Chase smiled. "That awesome Web site you designed is what's driving our business through the roof. That, and your contract with the Candle Corner, has our profit margin up twenty percent over last year."

He stopped in the doorway and smirked. "Just trying to make sure I earn my keep so the new owner doesn't throw me out on the street."

Chase laughed. Korey liked to tease him about being the new owner, even though Chase was a couple of years away from buying out his cousin's share of the family business. "I think you're safe, buddy." Then he sobered. Better give Korey the whole scoop before it broke on the news. "Guess I should tell you before you hear it somewhere else that I'm the one who found that body this morning."

Korey's eyes went round. "No kidding?"

Chase nodded.

"Ah, man. I wondered where you were this morning." He paused. "Uh…what were you doing in the park?"

Chase lifted a shoulder. "Just walking. You know?"

Korey's gaze dropped to the floor in front of his feet. "Yeah. I know. If I can help, just ask."

It took a few seconds before Chase's throat loosened enough so that it was safe to answer. "Thanks. I appreciate that."

When Korey disappeared in the direction of the pouring room, the face of a stubborn police detective came into focus in Chase's mind. Was Irene right? Would Detective Jenkins uncover something that would help reveal what had really happened to Kevin?

He bounced a pencil eraser on the desk. Jenkins had refused to listen to reason last year, and nothing Chase saw this morning indicated he had changed. There had been times Chase wanted to grab him by the shoulders and shake some sense into him.

Maybe Chase could force him to listen to reason this time. Maybe if he offered to help the police, he could somehow help clear up the dirty rumors still circulating about Kevin's death.

Chase stood abruptly. The desk chair rolled into the wall behind him with a loud *smack*. What was he thinking? No way he was getting involved with another murder investigation. One was enough.

He tossed the pencil onto the desk and headed for the door. Numbers weren't going to hold his attention today. He'd go see if Alex could use some help with that pour.

THREE

A sign on the side of the road a couple of miles inside the Brown County line caught Caitlin's attention.

Good Things In Wax
Scented Candle Factory
Free Tours Monday Through Saturday
Closed Sunday
3 Miles ———>

She tilted her left hand on the steering wheel to see her watch. Just past one o'clock. Check-in time at the hotel wasn't until three. A tour might be a good way to kill some time. She turned in the direction the arrow indicated.

Three hours in the car with her favorite music blasting had improved her mood considerably. And she'd reached an important decision a few miles inside the Indiana border.

Who needed a guy to be happy? Not her. She had a job she loved teaching music to a terrific bunch of kids. She had her church activities, her friends, Sassy. Plenty to keep her occupied while she healed. And she needed time to heal, which was the reason she'd decided she needed a dateless year. She refused to let a romantic thought even cross her mind for at least twelve months. If God wanted her to go out on a date before then, He'd have to drop a guy on her doorstep with a bow around his neck.

After her big decision, the drive had been uneventful until she pulled off the interstate onto the four-lane road that would take her into Nashville. Or "Little Nashville," as a billboard proclaimed. The landscape in this part of the country boasted a beauty all its own. Dense trees blanketed the rolling Blue Hills of Indiana, though at this time of year they weren't very blue. Deep, pinkish-purple spring blooms covered the redbuds that grew in abundance throughout the woods on both sides of the road.

As promised, Good Things In Wax lay three miles off the main road. The Geo's tires crunched over a small gravel parking lot toward a charming wooden building with a wide covered porch. The building had no windows, except for the one in the front door. Caitlin parked and climbed out of the car.

The scent of vanilla warred with the natural smells of pine and soil from the surrounding forest. She drew in deep breaths as she mounted the steps to the porch. Vanilla was one of her favorite scents.

The moment she stepped inside, a mishmash of odors and colors assaulted her senses. She stood in the factory's gift shop, where hundreds of multihued candles lined shelves on all four walls. The door whooshed closed behind her, and for a moment she didn't move, but let her gaze sweep the room as she adjusted to the sensory overload. She imagined there were at least fifty different varieties of candles—pillars, tapers, and candles in jars. The combination of scents, with the un-mistakable smell of hot wax dominating the rest, was almost overpowering. How could people work in here all day? Maybe they eventually got used to it.

To her right stood a sales counter with a cash register and a rack of flyers. No sales clerk, though. She glanced at one of the brochures, a promotional piece about the company and a list of their most popular scents. A sign beneath the glass on the counter listed the prices for each size and announced, "Buy Three And The Fourth Is Free!"

She had just picked up a deep-maroon jar candle off the closest shelf when someone came through the doorway in the rear wall behind her.

"Hello. Feel free to look around and I'll be happy to answer any questions."

"Okay, thanks." She half turned to smile at the man as she pried off the lid. When she caught sight of him, she stopped, the candle momentarily forgotten.

A friendly smile flashed in her direction as he pulled a wax-splattered canvas apron off over a head with hair the color of ripe wheat. His shirt shifted upward over a trim waist when he raised his arms. She tore her gaze away quickly as he folded the apron and tossed it on the corner of the sales counter.

And then she glanced back at his left hand.

Oh, no! I've turned into one of those desperate women who checks for a wedding ring! I can't stand those women!

A stab of anger sent heat flooding through her. Her decision to embrace her single status wasn't two hours old, and here she was, ogling the ring finger of the first handsome guy she came across.

This is Glenn's fault. The bum. Look what he's turned me into.

Well, she refused to become one of *those* women.

A full year without dating. I mean it.

"That's a good one."

Caitlin realized she'd been staring at his hand. Her gaze jerked upward to his face. "Excuse me?"

He nodded toward the jar she held. "Mulberry is one of our most popular scents."

"Oh." She pulled the lid off and raised the candle to her nose. "Mmm, that is nice. Kind of fruity."

"Well, berries *are* considered fruit." He grinned as he came around the counter toward her.

Was he flirting with her? A warm blush threatened to climb into her cheeks. Caitlin fought it off. He was a salesman, that's all. Trying to impress her with candles was his job.

"So they are." Caitlin busied herself with another deep sniff.

"Here, try this one." He picked up a light green jar, popped the lid off, and held it toward her. "It's Fresh Apple."

She leaned forward to inhale the candle's aroma. "Ah, that's nice. Smells just like real apples."

His smile lit his eyes. "Glad to hear it. We try hard to keep the scents authentic."

The front door burst open and a woman bustled through.

"Chase, I'm so sorry I'm late. I was just going to dash into the bank, but I ran into Helen from church and I couldn't get away from her. Seems like the whole town is talking about that body in the park. Oh." She noticed Caitlin and raised a hand to cover her mouth, eyes round. "Sorry, honey," she said to Chase.

Body? Caitlin cast a startled glance at the man this woman had just called "honey." His lips formed a tight line as he repositioned the Fresh Apple candle on the shelf.

"Anyway," the woman rushed on, "here's the receipt from the deposit." She fished a slip of paper out of her purse and set it on the counter. A bright smile widened her mouth as she turned toward Caitlin. "Hello. I'm Betty Hollister."

Caitlin opened her mouth to answer, but Chase beat her.

"This is my mother."

"Your mother?" Actually, now that she looked closer, Caitlin could see a family resemblance in the shape of their eyes.

They both grinned. "Good Things In Wax is a family business," Mrs. Hollister explained. "Though my sister and I mostly just assist these days. Chase and his cousin Korey are the next generation, and they're the real brains behind the business."

What a nice thing to say. Motherly pride beamed from her eyes as she turned toward her son. Caitlin smiled warmly at her.

Chase ignored the compliment, but moved his pointer finger across the shelf as he scanned the labels. "Were you looking for a particular scent?"

Ah. Back to business. "Actually, no. I just got into town and saw your sign out on the main road."

"I didn't think you were from around here," Mrs. Hollister said. "I hear an accent in your voice."

Chase cocked his head and eyed her speculatively. "South, I'd guess. But not too far south. Kentucky, or maybe Tennessee?"

"You're good. Kentucky." Caitlin confessed, "I don't like my accent. I wouldn't mind sounding like a southern belle, but I'm afraid I'm more like a hillbilly."

Mrs. Hollister laughed. "I think it's charming."

Caitlin liked the woman. Something about her laugh was infectious. But then she caught a calculating sparkle in the eyes that swept from her to Chase. Uh-oh. Something of a matchmaker for her son, was she?

Sorry, Mrs. Hollister. You'd better keep looking. I've got three hundred sixty-five days of unencumbered singleness ahead of me.

Caitlin cleared her throat. "I saw on your sign that you give free tours, and thought I might take one." She glanced around the room, looking for a listing of the tour times. "When is the next one scheduled?"

Mrs. Hollister looked at her watch. "How does right now sound?"

"Perfect. Do you conduct the tours?"

The woman looped her hand through her son's arm and squeezed. "Chase does a much better job with the tours than I do. He can tell you everything you ever wanted to know about candle making."

Chase looked startled. "But I've got to finish the invent—"

"Nonsense!" The stern look Mrs. Hollister turned on her son brought a grin to Caitlin's face. She looked like she was scolding her ten-year-old, though Chase was closer to thirty, if Caitlin was any judge.

"I don't want to be any trouble," Caitlin said. "I'm here until Sunday night. I could come back tomorrow."

The stern look turned her way. "It's no trouble at all. Is it, Chase?"

He obviously didn't want to be bothered giving her a personal tour. But apparently he wasn't up for contradicting his mother. The smile he assumed held a touch of resignation. "I have been making candles long enough to know a thing or two about the process."

This is a joke, isn't it, God? Throw me together with a handsome guy, add a few not-so-subtle nudges from his mother—it's a test to see if I'm really serious about my decision, isn't it?

Well, Caitlin was accustomed to scoring well on tests.

"That's terrific. Thanks so much." Did her voice sound too bubbly, too enthusiastic? To cover her embarrassment, she thrust her hand toward him. "My name's Caitlin Saylor."

"Nice to meet you, Caitlin."

Their hands connected, and the soft skin of Caitlin's palm tingled where it nestled next to his. An answering flutter tickled the pit of her stomach. This kind of stuff never happened to her. Why now, *after* her decision?

When Chase released her hand, she clutched the shoulder strap of her purse and lifted her chin, determined to ignore the flutter.

Three hundred and sixty-five days. No problem.

"We break the blocks into smaller pieces to speed the melting process." Chase directed Caitlin's attention to the worktable where Alex stood hacking at a slab of wax with a hammer and chisel.

She stopped her curious inspection of the room to watch Alex. Chase didn't think her interest was feigned, though up in the shop he'd thought she might hightail it out of there when his mom started shoving them together.

Not that Chase would have blamed Caitlin. In fact, he'd have been tempted to flee with her, to escape the machinations of his mother when she got that gleam in her eye. And she seemed to get it a lot lately. Like finding him a date had become her number-one priority in life or something. She reminded Chase at least twice a week that he hadn't gone on a date since he and Leslie broke up, shortly after Kevin's death.

The image he'd seen inside the car this morning flashed across his mind with surprising clarity. An answering surge of bile threatened. Chase gulped in a couple of deep breaths.

"I do the same thing with baker's chocolate." Caitlin brought him back to the task at hand. "Otherwise part of it scorches before the bigger pieces have a chance to melt."

"Exactly."

Alex pounded off another chunk, this time with a quick

sideways glance at Caitlin as the piece of pale white wax broke off. Were his biceps bulging more than normal? Yeah, they were. Chase swallowed a disgusted grunt. Alex was flexing them on purpose, the show-off. Known as something of a lady's man, Alex loved to put on a show for the pretty tourists.

And Caitlin was pretty. Blond hair. Blue eyes. The top of her head was on level with his nose.

Her looks weren't lost on Alex, apparently. The guy puffed his chest out and swaggered behind the table where he stood. "This is the easy part," Alex said. He waved a dismissive hand at the block of wax. "Requires nothing but brute force." The show-off gave her a broad wink as he hefted a new slab of wax into position. "Stick around and I'll be happy to demonstrate the part that takes finesse a little later."

Judging by the way her cheeks flushed, she caught the double entendre. Chase couldn't tell if she was pleased or embarrassed by Alex's flirting, but she didn't meet his eyes. Definitely didn't flirt, like many women would have.

In fact, she hadn't flirted with him, either. Chase liked that—he preferred women who didn't go for all that eyelash-batting stuff.

"Thanks for the offer, but I think we're good." Chase gave Alex a stern stare over the top of Caitlin's lowered head. Grinning, the Romeo lifted a shoulder and picked up his hammer.

Chase smiled down at Caitlin. "Let's go into the other room, where the *real* work takes place."

He put a hand on the back of her arm and guided her away from Alex's worktable. He pointed out the neat rows of twenty-five-pound pails containing scented oil, stored on shelves along the rear wall, then led her through the doorway into the long, narrow room beyond. Fifty or so jars filled with liquid wax lined the worktable in the center. At the deep sink,

Irene was cleaning up the last of the equipment from the morning's pour. She flashed a smile in their direction, continuing with her task.

"You just missed a pour," he informed Caitlin as he led her down the length of the table. "We did French Vanilla this morning."

He described the process of mixing the fragrances, achieving the correct wax temperature, securing the wicks and pouring, and also the various effects to be achieved by different cooling techniques.

When he finished his spiel, she pointed toward a table that lined the rear wall, laden with dozens of metal molds. "You do all kinds of candles at once? Jars, pillars, tins, all the ones I saw in the shop?"

He shook his head. "We use a different kind of wax for pillars and votives, because they have to be taken out of the mold." He nodded toward the table. "Those are Cinnamon Red Hots from yesterday afternoon. They're ready to be unmolded, wrapped and shipped out."

She gave him a surprised look. "Shipped out? You don't sell them all here?"

"Oh, no. The shop is just one small piece of our business. We have a great Web site, and we get orders from all over the country. And most of our local business comes from the shops downtown."

Chase led her to the third worktable, where four boxes of jar candles stood waiting for delivery. "These are interesting." He flipped open a flap of the box and pulled out a deep-purple candle. "Forbidden Fantasy. Last year we designed this scent for a shop here in town. They sell a ton of them."

He held the jar up for her inspection, and she read from the label. "'Made by Good Things In Wax exclusively for The Candle Corner, Nashville, Indiana.'" She tilted her head to look at him sideways, a smile hovering at the edge of her mouth. "So you mean I can't buy this from you? I'd have to go downtown to get it?"

That almost-smile was contagious. Chase found his mouth curving in answer, and was unable to look away from eyes almost exactly the same shade of blue as his favorite Maui Breeze candle.

On impulse, he pushed the jar toward her. "You don't have to go anywhere. This is your gift for taking the tour. With our compliments."

The smile broke loose, and a deep dimple creased her cheek. "Thank you."

Blue eyes, blond hair, dimples. Chase tore his gaze away, his throat suddenly dry. "That concludes the tour, I'm afraid. If you'll follow me."

"Hey!"

An exclamation from behind made Caitlin jump, and Chase turned, frowning toward the intruder. Willie Evans had come through the back door and was hovering at the edge of the worktable.

"Yes, Willie?" Chase kept his tone polite. Truth be told, he didn't like the man. Something about the way he wouldn't look Chase in the eye when they talked. Like now. His eyes moved continually, darting between Caitlin and Chase and the boxes of product. But he was a charity case of Korey's, who'd insisted on giving him a job as a part-time delivery driver because the guy needed steady employment. He was too scattered, too inattentive to trust in the factory, but he was a good driver. He'd never had an accident, and Chase had to admit, Willie was reliable. He showed up for work when he was supposed to and he made the deliveries on time.

"Uh, I was just getting ready to take those over to the Candle Corner." A muscle beneath his left eye twitched as his gaze fixed on the jar in Caitlin's hand. "Now there's one short. I don't wanna get in trouble or nothing."

Chase forced himself to smile at the man. "Don't worry. I'll make sure their account reflects the credit. If anybody says anything, have them call me."

Willie's tongue made an appearance to run quickly across his lower lip, his gaze fixed on the candle. His nod was more like a jerk. "I'll tell 'em."

Chase flashed a quick smile of dismissal before he turned away, and Caitlin fell in beside him. As they passed through the workroom, Alex stopped in the act of placing another slab of wax on the sturdy table to watch their progress across the room. Caitlin didn't seem to notice his attention, but stuck right by Chase's side, holding her candle close. Chase straightened his shoulders and smirked over the top of her head. *Take that, Casanova.*

FOUR

They stepped into the shop to find Chase's mother chatting with two older women. Caitlin hesitated. Should she buy something? It would probably be the polite thing to do, since she'd taken up so much of his time—and since he'd given her one candle as a gift already.

She turned away from him to hide a fit of nerves. The suddenness of his gesture in the back room led her to believe not every person who took the tour left with a gift. Especially one of the special candles they didn't even sell in their own store. That definitely counted as flirting. And she'd probably flirted back, despite her best intentions.

She straightened and infused her tone with politeness. "Thank you for that tour. And for this." She popped the lid off the candle, lifted it to her nose, and inhaled. "Mmm—"

Her throat closed off in a choke as the odor reached her nostrils. Or, rather, assaulted her nostrils. A pungent blend of eucalyptus and...was that licorice? Tears sprang to her eyes. Whatever it was, the combination was horrible.

"Oh." She replaced the lid, blinking rapidly to clear her eyes. The smell clung to the back of her throat. If Chase hadn't been standing there watching, she would have wrinkled her nose and coughed. "That's really strong."

"You don't like it?"

"Oh, no, it's not that," Caitlin hurried to assure him. "It's just that it's, uh…" She swallowed. What could she truthfully say about that terrible smell without offending him? "Really strong," she repeated lamely.

Though his expression was serious, laugh lines creased the edges of his eyes. "It is one of our strongest scents."

"Well, at least it's…" Caitlin held the jar up and peered at the dark purple wax. She'd been about to say, "At least it's pretty," but she wasn't a fan of purple. And this was so dark it was almost black. Black candles had such sinister connotations, she wouldn't dare display this one in her living room. She searched desperately for something nice to say.

"To be honest," Chase said, "it's not one of my favorites."

She caught sight of a twitch at the corner of his lips, and relaxed. "Mine, either," she confessed. "I'm more of a plain vanilla kind of girl."

He took the candle from her unresisting hands and tucked it on a shelf beneath the sales counter. "In that case, we have a triple-scented vanilla candle you're going to love."

Caitlin let him guide her toward a shelf on the opposite side of the shop, ignoring the warmth of his light touch at the small of her back. "You said the store in town sells a lot of those Forbidden Fantasy candles?"

"A ton."

She tried to keep the disbelief off her face, but apparently failed, because he held his hand out, palm up and fingers splayed, as he shrugged.

"I don't understand it, either." He lowered his voice and glanced at the three women on the other side of a display shelf. "Personally, I think they stink."

A giggle escaped her lips. Caitlin cut it off quickly. She might not be interested in the guy, but that didn't mean she wanted him to think she was one of those giggly women she couldn't stand. They were often the same ones who checked for wedding rings.

Chase didn't seem to mind. He picked up a jar filled with creamy white wax, twisted off the lid, and extended it toward her. "How's this?"

She inhaled, and breathed a happy sigh. "Wonderful. I love that one."

His smile deepened as he put it in her hands. "Good. We like to keep our customers happy."

Was there a bit of extra meaning in those words? Heat flooded Caitlin's face, and she tore her gaze away from his. "I think I'll buy one of those Fresh Apples you showed me earlier. My mom loves candles, and the green will match her bathroom perfectly."

Mrs. Hollister stepped behind the cash register to ring up the purchases of the pair of women she'd been helping. Caitlin took her place in line behind them while Chase wrapped her candles in thick paper. When the women left with bulging bags clutched in their hands, Mrs. Hollister turned her wide grin on Caitlin.

"And how did you like the tour, dear?"

"It was fascinating. I never knew the process of making candles was so involved."

The woman locked her arm through Chase's and beamed up at him. "Chase is going to own the whole company some day."

"Mother." He gave her a stern look and extracted his arm.

Caitlin hid a smile as she took her wallet from her purse. She handed Chase enough money to cover the total displayed on the register's screen.

"So, how long are you in town?" Mrs. Hollister asked.

"Until Sunday afternoon. My friends and I have a musical

trio and we're playing at a wedding Saturday evening, but I came up a few days early."

"You're here alone?"

Caitlin could almost see the thoughts flying back and forth behind the woman's arched eyebrows. Uh-oh. She knew what came next. Better halt this conversation right now, or she'd find herself fending off an invitation to their house for a big family dinner.

"My friends couldn't get off work until Friday, but I decided to come a few days early to spend some time in prayer and bible study. You know, a kind of retreat." She raised her eyebrows. "Alone."

That made Mrs. Hollister pause.

Chase cut into the conversation, his tone holding a note of polite dismissal. "Thanks for taking some of your retreat time to visit our factory." He extended the bag across the counter toward her, his smile friendly. "We hope you have a nice time in Little Nashville."

Caitlin took the bag, more than willing to be dismissed. The sooner she got out of Mrs. Hollister's calculating presence, the better. "I'm sure I will. Thank you for the tour, and the candle."

She turned to go, and Mrs. Hollister practically ran around the counter. "Wait! Since you're here on a retreat, you should come to our church tonight."

Caitlin paused. "Your church?"

The woman's eager smile deepened as she nodded. "We're having a miniconcert tonight instead of our regular Wednesday service. One of the local gospel groups is performing. I really think you'd enjoy it, especially since you're a musician yourself."

Caitlin's interest sparked to life. She loved gospel music. "That does sound good."

"Excellent!" Mrs. Hollister put a hand on Caitlin's arm.

"The concert is at seven-thirty, so how about coming to dinner at our house around six?"

Ah. There it was. As expected.

Chase stood silent behind the register, his lips pressed into a tight line. He didn't want Caitlin at his family's dinner table any more than she wanted to be there. A completely unreasonable stab of disappointment assaulted her at the realization.

Caitlin took a step toward the door, beyond the woman's clutch. "Thank you, but I'd better not come for dinner. Tell me where your church is, and I might come to the concert."

Mrs. Hollister was nothing if not determined. "Oh, it's much too complicated for you to try to find on your own. Chase will pick you up. Where are you staying?"

Caitlin opened her mouth to protest, but Chase stopped her.

"Actually," he said, "our church is off the beaten path. It might be best if I gave you a ride. That is, if you plan to come."

Klaxon alarms sounded in Caitlin's ears. Her heart was vulnerable, and she knew it. The pain inflicted by Glenn was too fresh, too raw. That's why the dateless year was so important. She needed time to heal so she wouldn't fall head over heels for the first good-looking guy who came along. And Chase definitely fit that mold.

But this wasn't really a date, was it? It was a concert at church. No harm in that, surely.

"I'm staying at the Nashville Inn," she told Chase.

"I'll pick you up around seven, then." His gaze fixed on something behind her. A half-formed smile froze on his lips.

Caitlin turned and looked through the window in the door. A vehicle pulled into the space next to her Geo, white with green lettering and the unmistakable red-and-white bar across the top. A cruiser from the Brown County Sheriff's Department.

"It's the police." Mrs. Hollister's voice was low. "What do they want?"

"Me." Chase stared out the window. "They want me."

Startled, Caitlin jerked her head around to stare at him. The police were here for the handsome candle man?

What have I gotten myself into?

FIVE

Chase stood in the parking lot beside Detective Jenkins's vehicle and watched Caitlin's car disappear down the tree-lined street. She was an attractive woman with a sweet, appealing air about her that he didn't come across often. And she'd survived Mom's clumsy maneuvering with grace. Exactly the kind of woman who could coax him back into the dating world. But the sight of the sheriff sent her scurrying away like a frightened squirrel. Not that he blamed her.

He glanced toward the detective, who sat behind the wheel of his car with a cell phone held to his ear. Chase's hands tightened into fists. The hours he'd spent last year being questioned by Jenkins were still fresh in his mind. This morning had been easy compared to the investigation surrounding Kevin's death. And Chase had never been able to make any headway in prying out information that would help him understand the real reason behind Kevin's murder. The detective's accusations had gnawed at Chase since the moment he'd first uttered them. And the worst part was, Jenkins had hard evidence to back up his claims, evidence Chase couldn't ignore and couldn't begin to explain.

Blood tests didn't lie. At the time of his death, Kevin had been high on heroin.

The guy Chase had known since grade school, the one who had worked right alongside him at the candle factory, wasn't the clean, straight-up friend he'd always appeared to be. He'd fooled everyone, including Chase.

The car door opened. Jenkins's head appeared over the top, his gaze locked on to Chase as though daring him to turn away. Chase stood his ground and returned the hard stare without flinching.

"Hollister." The man left the car door open and came around it.

"Detective Jenkins." Chase managed an even if guarded tone. "I didn't expect to see you again so soon."

"You can count on seeing a lot of me until we solve this crime." A smile flashed onto Jenkins's face and disappeared just as quickly. "The team is still combing the area where you found the body. Judging from the tire tracks, the car was pushed down the embankment from approximately the same place as your buddy's last year. If the killer is the same person, and I have no doubt it is—" Jenkins's stare became hard "—we won't find anything to identify him or her inside the car."

So much for Irene's suggestion that this crime would lead to new evidence about Kevin. From the sound of things, they didn't expect to find the killer this time, either.

But why come all the way out here to tell him? Just to needle him?

Chase let out a slow breath before he spoke. "What do you want from me, Detective?"

"For the moment, information." His eyes narrowed. "Ever hear of a man named Lancaster?"

Chase felt pinned beneath Jenkins's searching stare. "Lancaster?" He searched his memory. "Doesn't ring a bell."

"You sure? George Walter Lancaster?"

"No. I don't know anybody named George."

"Ever hear Kevin Duncan mention someone by that name?"

Jenkins's stare hardened, as though he could pry a confession out of Chase. But there was nothing to confess. Whoever this Lancaster guy was, Chase didn't know him.

After a minute, Jenkins's gaze fell away. "I hoped you might have heard of him. Lancaster is the dead guy you found in the park this morning. He wasn't from around here, and there's no indication he was in town a year ago when your buddy was killed. But he does have ties to a heroin ring up in Indianapolis."

"Heroin." Nausea churned in Chase's gut. How he hated that word.

Jenkins nodded. "I talked to DEA up there. Seems they'd been watching him for a while. Got a couple of tips that Lancaster's responsible for some pretty powerful stuff that's been hitting the streets in that area. Black tar heroin, all the way from Mexico."

"Then why didn't they arrest him?"

"They never caught him with the goods. They were making progress, but he must have gotten wind that he was being watched. He disappeared a couple of weeks ago. Guess we know where he slithered off to."

"Slithered" was right. If there was anything Chase despised more than a drug dealer, he couldn't think of it. "So he came down here and got tangled up with the same person who killed Kevin last year."

Of course he did. Druggies stuck together, didn't they? Chase ground his foot into the gravel that covered the parking lot.

"Apparently." Jenkins cocked his head. "You sure you never heard of him?"

Chase stiffened. Was the detective insinuating that he hung

out in the same circles as heroin users? But in the next instant he wilted. As far as Jenkins was concerned, he did. He used to hang out with Kevin.

He swallowed. "I'm sure."

His answer seemed to satisfy the detective. With a brief nod, Jenkins rounded the cruiser. "I'll be in touch."

"Detective?"

Chase stopped him with a word before he slid into the seat. The man paused in the act of bending. Chase licked suddenly dry lips.

"Uh, if you need help with anything, I'm here. Just ask."

Jenkins's eyes narrowed. "What kind of help would you be able to give me, Hollister?"

Chase lifted a shoulder. "I don't know. Whatever. If I can help you track down the person who killed Kevin, I will."

The man studied him for a long moment. Chase shifted his weight, but held Jenkins's gaze. Finally the detective pulled his card case out of his pocket, extracted a card, and held it across the roof of the car. Chase took it.

Jenkins spoke. "If you hear anything that might give us a lead, call me. Otherwise, stay out of our way."

With a hard swallow, Chase nodded. Jenkins slid into the car and shut the door. The vehicle's tires crunched on the gravel as it backed up, turned around, and headed for the road. Chase stood, unmoving, and watched until it was out of sight. He examined the card in his hand. How much help could he be? He didn't know anything about drugs or drug dealers, and he certainly knew no one who could commit murder. But he'd keep his ears open and feed any helpful scraps of information to the detective. It was the least he could do for Kevin.

Detective Jenkins clutched the steering wheel as he drove toward headquarters. A long afternoon in the office lay ahead of him. A regular death resulted in a ton of paperwork—the load doubled with a violent murder. And then there were extra reports to be filed with the DEA folks, even though they hadn't found any illegal drugs on Lancaster's body. Still, after his conversation with Indianapolis, DEA would want to be informed.

He turned onto the main road, and passed the sign for Hollister's candle factory. Interesting development, Hollister offering to help, even though he obviously disliked Jenkins. Not that Jenkins blamed him. Things had gotten pretty rough between them last year, what with Hollister insisting his buddy was clean. Jenkins had finally been forced to lay out the facts, show him the labs. That had taken the wind out of his sails.

There was something about Hollister, something Jenkins couldn't quite put his finger on. He'd picked up on it last year, and again just now. The man was smart, no doubt about that. Something told Jenkins that Hollister was connected to this Lancaster slime. Jenkins had been a cop too long to ignore that niggling in his gut. He'd better keep an eye on Hollister.

SIX

Caitlin walked up the picturesque street, shopping bags swinging at her side. Hundreds of darling shops and art galleries lined the streets of Little Nashville. The sidewalks were crowded with samples of the wares for sale inside, everything from hand-carved wind chimes to intricate macramé planters overflowing with multicolored blooms. The Internet had described Nashville as an artist colony, and Caitlin could see why. This place was a craft lovers' paradise.

She'd checked into the hotel, dropped her stuff in the room, and then left to wander what seemed to be the town's main street. A hand-painted sign pointed the way to Antique Alley, and that was something she definitely didn't want to miss. Her checking account was going to take a hit during this trip, and she didn't even care.

But she did care about her feet. All these brick and cobbled walkways looked charming, but they were rough on the feet. She had slipped on a pair of sandals, but tomorrow she'd opt for her comfy, worn sneakers. Jazzy would be horrified at the breach of fashion etiquette, but Jazzy wasn't here, was she? Caitlin put more stock in comfort than show.

Of course, she'd take extra care with her appearance tonight. It wouldn't do to look shabby when Chase picked her up for church.

She came to a halt on the sidewalk at the traitorous turn her thoughts had taken. *Tonight is not a date.*

So why then, had she mentally planned to wear the most flattering outfit she'd brought with her? She set her jaw. She *would not* violate the dateless year. Tonight was nothing more than a visit to church with a friendly stranger. And to prove it, she'd wear the orange sweater Jazzy said clashed with her blonde hair and made her look like a giant candy corn.

Besides, what was that policeman doing at the candle factory? Chase hadn't seemed at all surprised to see him. In fact, Caitlin had the definite impression that he'd expected the visit. Maybe there was a perfectly good explanation, but coming so soon after Mrs. Hollister's mention of a body, the sight of that police car raised a few red flags in Caitlin's mind. If she was going to be tempted to bend in her resolve, it wouldn't be because of someone who was even remotely involved with dead bodies and police officials. Even if her skin did tingle at his touch.

Her determination firm, she continued down the sidewalk. Up ahead she spied a shop sign that sounded familiar. The Candle Corner. That was the place that sold those horrible-smelling candles Chase's company made. Since she was right here, she might as well check it out.

A bell at the top of the door chimed as she pushed her way in. This place was far more crowded than the shop at Good Things In Wax. More than just candles filled these shelves. Shiny brass stands, colorful ceramic shades and trays, decorative metal holders, even lanterns—this shop sold anything remotely associated with candles, it seemed. There was a wide selection of candles from Good Things In Wax, and not just Forbidden Fantasy, she was glad to note.

Caitlin wandered down the first narrow aisle, holding her

bags carefully so they didn't knock into anything. Behind her, the bell chimed again as another customer came inside.

The young woman behind the sales counter, who had not spoken to Caitlin, perked up when she caught sight of the new customer. "Oh, hello, Mrs. Graham. Mr. Graham's in the back receiving a delivery from one of the suppliers. Do you want me to tell him you're here?"

"That's okay, Laura. We're not in a hurry."

Caitlin glanced toward the dark-haired woman. She must be the boss's wife. And the girl beside her was probably their daughter.

"Mom, I've got to get home." The girl's tone was anxious, her brow furrowed with worry. "The concert's tomorrow night. I've got to practice."

Caitlin's ears perked up. She understood all about preperformance jitters and wanting to get in as much practice time as possible.

She picked up a ceramic candle shade and looked at the sticker. Then she quickly put it back down. This store was a little too pricey for her tastes. She headed toward the rack of candles from Chase's company.

"Don't worry, Nicky. You've got all night to practice." The woman's voice drew nearer as she made her way down the aisle next to Caitlin. "Look at these tea lights. They must be new."

"They are," said the sales clerk. "They just arrived last week."

"Nicky, wouldn't they look adorable in your room?"

"I guess." Judging from Nicky's sulky voice, she wasn't in the mood for decorating.

Caitlin half listened as she scanned the shelves. There. Forbidden Fantasy was easy to pick out. It was by far the darkest candle here. She picked it up. This jar was smaller than the one Chase had given her. On impulse, she twisted off the lid. Surely it wasn't as bad as she remembered.

One whiff set her coughing and sputtering. As she clamped the lid back down on the jar, a low laugh sounded beside her.

"Not fond of that one?"

Caitlin tried to put on an apologetic expression as she faced the store owner's wife. "I'm sorry. I know it's a special fragrance for this store."

The woman raised her hands, palms toward Caitlin. "Hey, don't apologize to me. I think it's awful myself."

Caitlin nodded her agreement. "I'm afraid I agree. Do people really buy it?"

The woman gave a short laugh. "A lot of them, apparently. My husband says he thinks it's mostly people who smoke or have a bunch of animals in their houses. Apparently it kills other strong smells."

"I believe it."

The girl hovered behind her mother, an anxious frown tugging at her mouth. She looked about twelve or so, long-legged and rail thin with straight dark hair tucked behind her ears.

Caitlin smiled at her. "I couldn't help overhearing earlier. You're playing in a concert tomorrow?"

A quick, dark-eyed glance in Caitlin's direction, and then the girl gave a shy nod and half turned away.

Her mother's face lit with pride. "It's the school band's last concert of the year, and the first chair has come down with the flu. Nicole just got a big solo, her first."

"That's wonderful." Caitlin addressed the girl. "What instrument do you play?"

"Flute," came the mumbled reply.

"Really?" Caitlin didn't bother to filter the delight out of her tone. "I play the flute, too."

That brought the girl's gaze back to her. "You do?"

Caitlin nodded. "I'm in town because I'm playing in a

wedding this weekend. I'm a flute teacher. I teach flute and piccolo back home in Kentucky."

Nicky's eyes widened to twice their normal size. "Do you think you could give me a lesson?"

"Nicky! Don't be rude." The girl's mother scolded her with a stern look. "I'm sure she doesn't have time to give you a lesson."

"But it would only take a few minutes." Nicky turned a pleading glance toward Caitlin. "I'm not very good, and I just know I'm going to blow the whole thing."

In the face of Nicky's worried expression, Caitlin hated to turn her down. Many of her students were that age, so full of middle-school angst that a solo they weren't prepared for could feel like the end of the world. And now that she thought about it, giving a lesson to an anxious girl might be the perfect excuse to cancel with Chase.

No, she'd feel like a heel. Mrs. Hollister would be beside herself. Caitlin had said she'd go, and she would. Besides, she really was looking forward to an evening of gospel music.

Caitlin was saved from answering Nicky's plea by the appearance of a man through a doorway in the corner. Irritation clipped his words short as he spoke to the clerk. "Laura, do you have any idea where I left my glasses?" His irritated expression deepened when he caught sight of Nicky's mom. "Janie, what are you doing here? I'm working."

Now it was Janie's turn to look worried. She flashed a quick, almost embarrassed smile in Caitlin's direction and then placed a hand on her husband's arm. "We came to tell you some good news, Ed. Nicky has a solo in tomorrow night's concert. Isn't that great?"

Ed's gaze flickered toward his daughter for an instant before he asked impatiently, "What concert?"

"The band concert at school." Janie's voice lowered. "You remember. It's the last one of the year."

"Oh, yeah. Right." He put a hand on top of Nicky's head and gave it a quick rub. "That's great, sweetheart. Congratulations." He glanced toward the door he'd just come through, then spoke to his wife. "I might not be able to make it, though. Be sure to take the camcorder, okay?"

Nicky looked at the floor, the corners of her lips twitching downward. Caitlin's heart twisted in sympathy. Her arms itched to comfort the girl with a hug. Or her mother, who looked just as stricken as Nicky.

"You'll try though, won't you, Ed?"

"Yeah, sure. Of course I will." He seemed to register Caitlin's presence at that moment. A wide smile transformed his features as he gestured toward the candle in her hands. "Are you finding everything okay?"

It was all Caitlin could do to reply pleasantly, when she'd much rather march him into the back room and give him a good talking to about paying an appropriate amount of attention to his sensitive preteen daughter. "I am. Thank you."

"Good, good. If you need anything, Laura will be happy to help you."

As though on command, the sales clerk appeared at his side holding a pair of reading glasses. "You left them up front."

"Thanks." He took them and gave Nicky's head a final rub. "I gotta get back to work. I'm having an inventory problem with one of the suppliers."

As he disappeared through the doorway into the back, Caitlin made a snap decision. She glanced at her watch. "I've got about half an hour. Just enough time for a lesson."

The girl lifted her head, hope flooding her face. "Really?"

Janie's look was full of gratitude. "Our house is just around the corner. You can follow us over, or I'll take you back to your car when you're through, if you prefer."

"Since I'm parked all the way down at the other end of town, that'll be faster."

"Then let's go!" Nicky headed toward the door at a jog, anxious not to waste any more lesson time.

Caitlin started to follow, and Janie stopped her with a hand on her arm. "Thank you."

Any regret Caitlin might have had about her impromptu decision fled at the sight of grateful tears in Janie's eyes. Without a doubt, this was an opportunity from the Lord's hand. The small act of kindness she could show this woman and her daughter was worth the minor interruption of her shopping spree. Given the glimpse she'd just had of Ed, they weren't accustomed to kindness.

She squeezed the woman's warm hand. "I'm happy to do it. Really."

She might have to forgo a shower before Chase arrived to pick her up, but she wasn't going to dress up for him, anyway. Right? Right.

Glasses perched on the end of his nose, Ed scanned the inventory list. A turbulent storm of unease churned in his stomach. What did it matter if every other item on the list was accounted for? That one missing candle could ruin everything.

"You'd better take care of this, Willie."

The fidgeting deliveryman from Good Things In Wax wouldn't meet his gaze. Standing in the open doorway with his hands shoved deep into the pockets of his baggy pants, he scuffed a foot on the doorjamb. "The boss said he'd take care of it."

Ed scribbled his name at the bottom of the form, his teeth grinding against each other. "We can't let that candle go. I don't care what it takes, you've got to get it back."

Willie shook his head. "But the boss said—"

Ed thrust the clipboard into the man's chest so hard he

stumbled backward. "You really are a moron, aren't you? Don't you understand? Hollister's lame attempt to impress a woman could ruin us. If she burns that candle, we're going down. Hard."

Willie did meet his gaze then. A muscle twitched in his cheek. "I can't go back to jail."

Fear filled his eyes as he spoke. Good. Ed didn't want to be the only terrified man involved in this mess. "Then you'd better do whatever it takes to get that candle back."

"I can't do nothing." Willie's throat convulsed as he gulped. "I don't even know who the lady was. I never saw her before."

Ed slitted his eyes. "You'd better find out. Fast."

"But the boss—"

Ed cut him off with an impatient gesture. "I don't care what he said. Ask Hollister who the girl was. Make up some excuse, say she looked familiar or something. If you're smart about your questioning, you might even be able to dig up something helpful, like where she's staying." Even as he said it, Ed knew *smart* wasn't an adjective anyone ever used to describe Willie. But what choice did he have? At this point, he had to use any resource he could to find that candle.

From the increasing speed of Willie's twitch, Ed could tell he didn't relish the idea of questioning Hollister, but the man nodded and started to turn in the open doorway. Then he stopped.

"Hey! That's her. That's the girl with the candle."

Ed looked toward the other end of the parking lot where Willie pointed. What he saw twisted his gut into instant knots.

Hollister's girlfriend was the blond customer who'd just been shopping in his store. She unwittingly held his fate in her possession. And she was getting into the car with his wife and daughter.

SEVEN

The afternoon's schedule kept Chase too busy to dwell on Detective Jenkins's questions. He and Irene did a pour of three dozen Freesia jar candles, followed by a batch of Georgia Peach pillars that made him think of Caitlin's charming southern accent.

He'd just finished setting the last pillar mold on the cooling table when Alex entered the workroom.

"You seen Korey?"

Chase shook his head as he helped Irene gather their tools from the table and take them to the sink for cleaning. "He's probably involved in some woodworking project or other. You know how he is."

When their grandfather ran the factory, the old man used to hound Korey to stop wasting so much time "playing with wood" and focus on the family business. But Korey loved working with wood in a way that he'd never loved candle making. And he had a way with wood, just like he had a way with computers.

"Yeah, he's probably busy whittling a toy train or something." Alex stuck a thumb through a belt loop and eyed Chase with a sly look. "So, did you score a date with that girl on the tour this afternoon?"

Chase set the tools on the counter and smiled his thanks to Irene, who started to fill the sink with hot, soapy water. He answered Alex without looking at him. "Not exactly a date."

A scowl compressed Alex's features. "What do you mean, 'not exactly a date'? Are you going out with her or not?"

Chase glanced at him. Did he detect a hint of jealousy in their resident Don Juan's attitude? "We're going to church to hear a gospel group."

Alex stared with disbelief. "Are you kidding? A looker like that, and you ask her to go to *church* with you?" He shook his head. "You religious types blow my mind."

Chase picked up a scraper and attacked the stray drops of hardened wax that had dripped onto the worktable. "Taking a girl to church is a lot better than hanging out in a smoky bar, if you ask me. Maybe you ought to try it sometime, Alex."

"Me?" Alex's shoulders shook with laughter. "There's nothing I want in any church."

Chase scraped at the table without looking up. He'd been over this ground before. The guy left very few openings for Chase to share his faith. He'd learned to keep the conversation light, or risk turning Alex off completely. Better to scatter a few seeds here and there, and then pray for the Lord to send water in His time.

"I don't know about that," he said. "You might be surprised at what you'd find there."

Cynicism stole over Alex's face. "Yeah? Like what?"

"Well, for instance, at *my* church tonight, you'll find a cute little blonde." Chase grinned. "With me."

Irene, arms up to the elbows in soapy water, remained silent, but Chase saw her mouth curl with amusement when Alex issued a disgusted snort and left the room.

Chase's pickup rolled to a stop at a red light. He'd left the factory earlier than usual, giving his mom the excuse that he wanted to get home in time to shower and change before picking Caitlin up. Truth was, he couldn't concentrate. The image of the body in the car kept looming in his mind, and the monotonous task of candle making had failed to distract him. He had to get out of there, get moving.

Problem was, his thoughts came with him.

George Walter Lancaster, a drug dealer from Indianapolis. What was he doing in Nashville? Did he have connections here? Drug buddies? And were they the same people from whom Kevin had bought heroin?

The light changed to green, and Chase took his foot off the brake. The pickup rolled forward.

He knew nothing about the drug scene. Until Kevin's death and those lab results, Chase hadn't even been aware that heroin was available in Little Nashville. "Ignorance is bliss," the saying went. Well, not when it punched you in the gut with the death of your friend.

The worst part was the guilt. He'd been too involved with his own life and his plans with Leslie, and had ignored his friend. Over and over in his mind he'd replayed the times Kevin suggested that they get together for a game, or go grab a pizza. But Chase always had other plans, and hadn't been willing to change them. If he had, maybe Kevin would have confessed his problems. Maybe he could have helped.

And yet, he still had a hard time believing Kevin could hide something as serious as drug use. Nobody suspected. Not his family. Not Mom or Korey or Aunt Dot or Irene, who worked side by side with him at the factory every day. Those lab results had stunned them all.

Chase's hand tightened on the steering wheel. It just didn't make sense.

A line of police cars in front of an apartment building up ahead drew his attention. Four of them. Unusual to have so many in one place. As he drove slowly by, the building door opened and a cluster of uniformed officers and one man in a suit and tie exited. One of them carried a blue plastic container, identical to the ones his mother stored her scrapbooking stuff in. Following him, Chase caught sight of a familiar face.

Detective Jenkins.

Just as Chase's foot was about to stomp on the gas pedal for a quick escape, Jenkins looked up. Their eyes met. Chase let out the breath he'd been holding. He'd been spotted.

Talking to the detective three times in one day definitely wasn't high on Chase's list of things to do, but if he sped away, surely it would look suspicious. It would look like he was following the guy, watching him, and hoping not to be seen. Better to stop and prove that he had nothing to hide.

He swept his pickup to the curb in front of the first cruiser and hopped out. The group of officers approached.

"What are you doing here, Hollister?" Jenkins watched him through narrowed eyes.

Chase lifted a shoulder. "I'm on my way home. I saw all the cars and was curious."

"Hmm."

Jenkins didn't sound convinced. He stared at Chase for a long minute, and Chase held his gaze without flinching. Finally, he pursed his lips and turned away.

The officer carrying the container passed by, heading toward the closest police car. Chase glanced inside. Dozens, maybe hundreds, of small, shiny packets lined the bottom. His stomach soured.

"Is that drugs?"

The young officer standing beside Jenkins nodded. "Heroin. About twenty-thousand-dollars' worth."

The detective shot him a look full of warning, and the officer's mouth snapped shut.

Chase watched as the container was loaded in the back seat of one of the police cars. "Looks like you just ruined some drug dealer's day." The idea gave Chase a sense of grim satisfaction. That was twenty-thousand-dollars' worth of drugs off the streets of his town.

Jenkins's jaw tightened. "Trust me. His day was already ruined." He didn't meet Chase's gaze, but stared at the building.

Understanding dawned. "That's where Lancaster lived?"

Jenkins gave a single nod. He cocked his head, his stare intense. Chase turned to look at whatever claimed the detective's attention. All he saw was a brick, two-story apartment building with shutterless windows in neat lines on either side of a red wooden door. Not a soul in sight.

"Did you find anything else in there?" he asked.

Chase didn't really expect Jenkins to answer, and he didn't.

The younger officer standing beside them shifted his weight from one shoe to the other. "You want me to do something else, Detective?"

"Yeah." Jenkins spoke without removing his gaze from the building. "Paperwork. A recovery like this results in tons of paperwork, Matthews."

A long, almost silent sigh escaped the deputy's lips. "Yes, sir."

Chase ducked his head to hide a grin. Apparently paperwork was not one of the deputy's favorite tasks.

Detective Jenkins turned suddenly. His hand rose, and he snapped his fingers in front of Chase's face. "Jelly beans!"

Chase took a half step backward. "Excuse me?"

"I said *jelly beans.*" Jenkins didn't wait for a reply, but whirled on his highly polished shoe and stomped toward one of the police cruisers.

Chase spoke to the man's retreating back. "That's what I

thought you said." He cast a look of inquiry toward Deputy Matthews.

The younger man lifted his shoulders. "Don't ask me. Maybe he's hungry."

Matthews headed for his own car, leaving Chase alone on the sidewalk. He inspected the building once again. Nothing remotely resembled jelly beans.

"Okay, let's hear it once more. But this time I want you to focus on abdominal support. That'll help you control the air arriving at the embouchure and give you a stronger tone."

They sat in Nicky's bedroom before a collapsible music stand. Caitlin tapped the beat with her hands as Nicky ran through her solo again, while her mother, on the bed, leaned against the headboard and listened. The room filled with a pure, clear tone from the girl's flute.

When she finished, she lowered her instrument and beamed.

"Excellent!" Caitlin joined Janie in applauding her effort. "You're going to nail that solo tomorrow."

Nicky sat straighter for a minute, but then her shoulders drooped. "It's easy here, with just you and me and Mom. But tomorrow night, in front of an audience…" She shook her head. "I'll probably choke."

"Don't talk like that," Caitlin scolded. "Think positively."

"I am positive." Gloom filled Nicky's tone. "I *will* choke."

Caitlin placed a sympathetic hand on the girl's arm. "The violinist in my trio has such horrible stage fright she used to get physically ill before every performance. One thing that helps her is to get her bearings before the performance starts. Spend some time practicing in the room where you'll perform."

The girl looked thoughtful. "The concert's in our gymnasium. Maybe I could go over my solo tomorrow after school."

Caitlin gave her a bright smile. "Perfect! Run through the piece a few times, get a feel of the performance space, and you'll be fine tomorrow night."

Nicky fixed a hopeful gaze on Caitlin. "Do you think you could come with me? You know, help me remember all the stuff you just taught me?"

Janie sat up on the bed. "Nicky, Caitlin's in town on vacation. It's not fair to ask her to spend her time working."

"But it's just for a few minutes." The girl's fingers tightened around the flute in her lap. "It won't take long, I promise."

Caitlin had no resistance against her pleading. How well she remembered her own first flute solo, when she'd been about Nicky's age. Facing an audience could be terrifying. A shy girl like Nicky needed every advantage she could get.

She smiled broadly. "I'd love to."

Air whooshed out of Nicky's lungs as she let out a screech of joy and launched herself out of her chair to throw her arms around Caitlin. "Thank you!"

Janie clasped her hands beneath her chin. "Are you sure? We don't want to impose on your time."

"I'm positive. And I might just come to the concert tomorrow night, too." Caitlin glanced at her watch. Chase would be coming to pick her up in about an hour. She steeled herself against the nerves fluttering in her stomach as she stood. "But I've got to get going. Do you mind running me back to my car now?"

"Of course. Just let me get my keys."

Caitlin followed Janie into the kitchen while Nicky continued practicing. A teenager with long, unwashed hair stood by the counter. The waistband of his ragged jeans sagged far down his rear, giving Caitlin an unwelcome view of several inches of blue-and-white boxer shorts. At their entrance he jerked around, obviously startled. Janie's purse lay open on the counter in front of him.

"Drew, what are you doing in my purse?" Janie's voice held a note of accusation.

The teen's eyes flicked toward Caitlin before he answered. "Looking for your keys. I need to use the car."

Janie drew herself up, bristling at the insolent tone. Caitlin looked away. If she'd talked like that to her mother when she was a teenager, she'd have been grounded for life.

But apparently Janie wasn't going to push the issue in front of Caitlin. Her tone remained even. "I'd appreciate it if you'd ask first, before you go through my purse."

Drew's eyes rolled upward. "Fine. Can I *please* use the car?"

Janie's lips tightened before she spoke. "No, you may not. This is my friend, Caitlin, and I'm driving her somewhere right now. Then I'm going to the grocery store to pick up a few things for dinner. When I come back, you may use my car."

Drew's arms flew up as he huffed, furious. "Man, this sucks. I'm gonna be late."

He stormed out of the room, brushing by Caitlin without a glance.

Janie gave an embarrassed half laugh. "Teenagers, huh?"

Caitlin didn't have to comment on the nature of rude teenagers, because at that moment the telephone rang. Janie picked it up.

"Hello?" She paused. "Yes, Ed, she's still here. We're just getting ready to leave, though." Another pause. "Okay, I will. Bye."

She hung up the phone and stood looking at it for a moment. "I don't know what's come over him today. I never hear from him until he comes home from work late at night. He's called three times in the last half hour." She gave a laugh and looked at Caitlin. "He wanted to make sure I pay you for your time today."

"Oh, no, you don't." Caitlin waved a hand in dismissal. "Forget it."

Janie tilted her head. "Are you sure? I mean, this is what you do for a living, right? I wouldn't dream of asking you to teach Nicky for free."

"I'm sure. I enjoyed it." She glanced in the direction of the bedroom. "She really is talented. I hope she stays with it all the way through school."

A proud smile hovered on Janie's face as her gaze followed Caitlin's. "I hope so, too."

Caitlin trailed Janie to the garage and slipped into her car. As Janie pulled out of their neighborhood heading toward town, they passed a dirty white van parked on the side of the road. Caitlin wouldn't have noticed it at all, except that it pulled out onto the street behind Janie's car.

A shiver of unease worked its way down her spine. Why did she have the eerie feeling that the van was following them? She glanced back. It was too far away to make out the person behind the steering wheel. But when Janie turned onto the main road, the van did, too.

"Is something wrong?" Janie asked. She glanced into the rearview mirror.

Traffic was heavier on this street than in Janie's neighborhood—the van was two cars back now. The buffer eased Caitlin's worries. She was imagining things. Mrs. Hollister's mention of a body and the policeman visiting Chase must have spooked her more than she realized, which was silly. Whatever the reason behind those things, it had nothing to do with her.

She turned a quick smile toward Janie. "No, nothing's wrong."

But tonight she was going to come right out and ask Chase about that policeman's visit. No doubt there was a perfectly reasonable explanation, and hearing it would put her mind at ease.

EIGHT

The congregation of Blue Hills Church turned out in droves to hear the Twyman Family Quartet croon their country gospel tunes. Cars filled the small parking lot, and men wearing reflective vests directed newcomers into an empty field next to the church. Excitement tickled in Caitlin's belly as she watched a stream of people file through the double doors of the midsize brick church. She told herself the excitement was all about the upcoming concert and not in any way connected to the handsome man at her side.

Chase steered his truck onto the grass as directed. "I knew there'd be a lot of people here, but I had no idea. We're going to burst the building's seams tonight."

"I've never heard of this group, but they must be pretty popular." Caitlin waited for the car next to her to roll to a stop before she reached for the door handle.

Chase stopped her. "Here, I'll get that."

For a moment Caitlin almost let him. It had been a long time since a man opened a car door for her.

Then she came to her senses. This was *not* a date. He had no business pampering her. She jerked open the door and jumped to the ground as he rounded the front of the truck.

Chase's eyebrows arched. "An independent woman, I see."

A blush threatened to heat her cheeks. She fought it down with sheer willpower. "Something like that."

His chuckle sent a thrill through her.

Stop it! Three hundred sixty-five days. That's what I said, and I meant it.

Chase guided her toward the building with that light touch on her back, which, she was pleased, did not send a tingle through her this time. But his hand felt comfortably warm.

"I hope we aren't too late to get a seat," he said.

"Maybe your mother will save us a place."

"She won't be here tonight."

Caitlin shot him a surprised look. "Why not?"

His gaze slid sideways. "Apparently she didn't want to intrude."

"Oh." Caitlin stepped ahead, away from his warm, guiding hand. *Great. She wanted us to be alone.*

But if that was Mrs. Hollister's intention, she would be disappointed. The place was packed. They joined a stream of people entering the building. As they stepped into the crowded narthex, Chase grabbed her hand and grinned down at her. "Don't want to lose you in the crowd."

Oh, Lord, this is not helping.

They found an empty spot halfway up the sanctuary in the center of a pew and crab-walked past the other occupants. Caitlin viewed the small space and flashed an apologetic smile at the African-American woman next to her.

"Why, Chase Hollister, who's this pretty girl you brought with you tonight?" The woman beamed up at her.

Chase performed the introductions. "Maude Jackson, I'd like you to meet Caitlin Saylor. She's visiting for a few days from Kentucky." Chase lowered himself to the pew and scooted over as far as he could to make room for her.

"Don't be shy, honey." The woman's voice boomed as she

patted the narrow, cushioned space between them. "You just sit right down here by Maude. I hope you're a gospel lover."

"Yes, ma'am, I am." Caitlin wedged in between Maude and Chase, trying to condense herself into the smallest possible space, but there was no avoiding the press of Chase's thigh against hers.

Maude nodded approvingly. "We're gonna hear us some good music tonight, praise God." She leaned sideways and whispered in a voice easily overheard by everyone in the vicinity. "My girl, she's in the back somewhere with my grandson on account of she's embarrassed of her momma. But I don't care. Don't see how a body can keep still when a good gospel group starts singing praises to the Lord."

Her wide smile was infectious. Caitlin's nerves, tightened by Chase's proximity, relaxed as she returned it.

When the Twyman brothers stepped up on the platform at the front of the sanctuary, Maude straightened to alert attention. The quartet crooned song after melodious song, while Maude clapped and moved every inch of her full-size figure to the beat. Caitlin soon gave up trying to avoid Maude's energetic elbows. The music was good, and Maude's enthusiasm as contagious as her smile. Before long Caitlin was clapping and singing along.

The concert ended with a powerful country gospel arrangement of "Amazing Grace" that had the whole congregation on their feet. As the last notes faded away, Maude caught Caitlin in a smothering hug and spoke to Chase over her shoulder. "You bring her back to worship with us again, you hear me?"

Caitlin avoided looking at Chase as she returned the hug, and then followed Maude out into the crowded center aisle, Chase close behind her. When they exited the church, Maude swept away toward the parking lot with a final wave, while Chase guided Caitlin to the grassy lot where his truck was parked.

The sun had long since dipped below the horizon and was now no more than a dim glow in the west as the truck sped down the road toward the hotel. An awkward silence settled in the cab. Caitlin searched for a way to bring up the topic of the police officer naturally, but failed. Finally, she decided the direct approach was the best.

She turned in the seat to face him. "What did that police officer want with you this afternoon?"

His lips tightened. She thought at first he might not answer, but then his chest rose with a slow breath before he spoke.

"I don't know if you've heard a news broadcast today, but a man was killed last night in the park not far from here."

Caitlin watched him closely. The light of the instrument panel reflected off of a tight jaw, and his hands clenched around the steering wheel. Strong hands. She went cold. *Is he a killer? Am I in danger?*

In the next instant, she dismissed the thought. Chase wasn't a killer. True, she'd just met him, but she'd watched him during that concert. His faith shone in his eyes as he sang along with the gospel songs. She couldn't believe someone with a heart for worship could also be a killer. Whatever was bothering him, it certainly wasn't guilt over having murdered someone.

"I heard your mom mention a body this afternoon."

He jerked a nod. "Well, I discovered it."

Caitlin drew in a noisy breath. "Oh, Chase! That must have been awful."

His lips twisted. "It was. The detective you saw was coming to tell me they'd identified the dead man, to see if I knew him."

"And did you?"

"No, but…" Caitlin stayed silent and waited for him to go on. After a long moment, he did. "Last year my best friend was killed in the same park. Same place, even. They're sure the person who killed this man is the same one who killed Kevin."

He took his eyes off the road to look at her for an instant. A battle raged in those depths. Compassion flooded Caitlin. Losing a close friend was bad enough. But to find a second victim must have opened up all the wounds that had begun to heal since that first tragedy. If pain like that ever healed.

"I'm so sorry." Useless words, but what else could she say?

"Thanks." His smile was full of sadness. "It gets worse. Turns out my friend was using drugs when he was killed. And today they found a bunch of heroin in the new victim's apartment." He shook his head slowly. "Apparently, my best friend was mixed up in some sort of drug ring, and I never knew. If I had paid more attention to him, maybe I could have helped him."

Caitlin studied his profile for a moment. Her heart twisted with the pain she saw beneath the handsome surface. This man didn't need a date. He needed a friend.

And that didn't violate the dateless year.

She put a hand on his arm, hoping to offer some comfort. "I'll pray for you."

"Thanks. I appreciate that." His head jerked toward her to flash a quick smile. "So." His voice held an unspoken plea to change the subject. "What do you have planned tomorrow?"

Caitlin settled back against the seat, willing to let the matter drop if that's what he needed. "I've been sent on a mission." His eyebrows rose, and she laughed. "A shopping mission. I'm supposed to be spying out the best places to take my friends this weekend."

"You've got your work cut out for you. If there's one thing Little Nashville has more of than country music bands, it's shops."

"Yes, I saw that today." She adjusted the air vent so it didn't blow in her face. "Oh, I meant to tell you. You'll never guess who I met today. The wife and daughter of the owner of the Candle Corner."

"No kidding?" He navigated a wide curve in the road with both hands on the steering wheel. "Where did you meet Ed Graham's family?"

"I went into the store to see if they really did sell those terrible-smelling candles." They exchanged a smile. "Janie and Nicky were in there, and it turns out Nicky is playing a flute solo in her band concert tomorrow night. Since I'm a flute teacher, one thing led to another." She shrugged. "I went over to her house this afternoon and gave her a quick lesson."

He took his eyes off the road a moment to turn a surprised glance her way. "You gave a kid you don't even know a lesson on your vacation?"

Caitlin looked away from his stare, embarrassed. "Well, she was nervous. I remember my first flute solo and how scared I was. I wanted to help her. I even promised I'd go to the concert tomorrow night at the middle school."

"I played the drums in middle school." A little-boy grin twitched at his lips. "Mom didn't approve. I think she worried I'd run off to join a rock-and-roll band."

Caitlin relaxed against the seat back. "Yet you became a candle man instead."

He cocked his head toward her and confessed, "I wasn't a very good drummer." He slowed down, then steered the truck into the hotel parking lot. "You know, I haven't been to a band concert in years."

Was he hinting for an invitation to come with her? She dug in her purse for the hotel key card. *Lord, this is so not funny.* How many guys were willing to suffer through band concerts? And why couldn't she have come across this one *next* year? "Middle school bands are notoriously bad."

"Except I hear there's going to be an awesome flute soloist." He grinned. "We could grab some dinner first. Let's say around si—"

She cut him off with a gasp as her gaze strayed beyond his face. "Oh, no."

"What?" He whipped around in his seat.

Caitlin grabbed at the door handle, jerked it open, and leaped out of the truck. She ran toward her car, nausea stirring in her stomach. Her shoes crunched on glass.

The passenger window of her car had been shattered.

NINE

"I can't believe this." Caitlin's voice choked as she stood near the front bumper of Chase's truck, arms hugging her stomach. The red-and-blue lights from two police cruisers flashed on the splintered glass that still protruded from the bottom edge of the window frame. Tears slipped from her eyes to roll down her cheeks, and she dashed them away. "Just look at my car!"

Chase stood beside her, his hands shoved deep into his pockets. "Don't worry, Caitlin. It's just a window. Those are easy to fix."

Caitlin sniffed. "But it's my car." She glanced sideways at him. He probably thought her foolish for being upset about the shattered window of her ten-year-old Geo. But she'd bought that car brand new, her first, and she loved it. Besides, it got terrific gas mileage, and these days that counted for a lot. And the body was in great shape, too.

Except, of course, for the busted-out passenger window.

But her feelings of discomfort went far beyond the damage to her beloved car. Someone had violated her, rifled through her possessions. The shopping bags she'd left on the passenger seat were scattered about, the items they'd contained thrown to the floor. The glove compartment was open. Had the person who did this opened the door and sat in her car as he pawed through her things? A shudder rippled through her.

"Listen," Chase said, "I know a guy with a body shop who can fix that window. I'll give him a call first thing in the morning if you want."

She drew a shuddering breath. She had to get herself under control. Forget this obsessive imagining. Focus instead on getting the car fixed and moving forward.

She forced a smile and turned toward Chase. "Thank you. I appreciate that."

A police officer approached, a clipboard and pen in his hand. "We found a couple of partial prints on the door handle, but nothing clear enough to run an identification scan." He squinted as he peered into Caitlin's face. "You're sure nothing is missing?"

She swallowed. "I don't think so. I didn't buy much today, just a few odds and ends. A couple of embroidered hand towels, a coffee mug for my dad. My most expensive purchase of the day was a handbag from that quilt shop downtown. Those things are all still there." She shook her head. "I don't understand what the thief was after if he didn't take any of those things."

The officer made a note on his form as he answered. "Probably saw the shopping bags on the seat and decided to look for something he could sell." He gave her a stern look over the top of his glasses. "You really shouldn't leave things visible inside a car. It's an invitation for a break-in."

He thought the break-in was *her* fault? Caitlin stiffened. "I shouldn't have to worry when I lock things in my own car. People ought to have more respect for other people's property."

"They *ought* to, but I'm afraid many of them don't." Chase glanced around the parking lot. "I don't see any security cameras."

The police officer shook his head. "There aren't any external cameras, and the hotel staff didn't see a thing. This part of the parking lot isn't in visual range of the lobby."

"Any other witnesses?" Chase scanned the windows in the two-story building. Caitlin followed his gaze. The curtains were shut in every one, the outlines illuminated by indoor lights in only a couple.

"We're going to leave a note in the lobby for anyone who saw anything suspicious to give us a call." The officer's tone told Caitlin he didn't expect much of a response.

"Maybe it was just an act of vandalism. Kids out causing trouble for kicks." Chase pointed toward the edge of the building, just a few feet beyond his truck. "It would be pretty easy for somebody to slip around the side of the building with a baseball bat or a tire iron, bash in the window, and run."

"Whoever it was took the time to go through the interior," the officer pointed out. "But that doesn't mean it wasn't kids looking for something valuable to steal. That'd be my guess."

Caitlin looked at the corner of the building, and the darkness beyond. She nodded. "When they realized all they were going to get was a coffee mug and a couple of towels, they left in disgust."

The officer finished writing on his clipboard and peeled off a copy of the form. He handed it to Caitlin. "You'll need this for your insurance company. We'll give you a call if anything else develops."

"Thanks." Caitlin took the form and folded it in half. If she heard anything further from the officer, she'd be surprised.

She stood beside Chase and watched as both cruisers pulled away. The flashing lights went dark as they exited the parking lot.

Chase pulled his hands out of his pockets. "I think I've got some cardboard we can use to block that window for the night."

She followed him to the back of the pickup, where he raised the bed cover and pulled out an empty box with the candle company logo on the side. He rummaged in a toolbox and came up with a roll of duct tape. Caitlin watched as he cut a side panel from the box with his pocketknife and fitted it in place of the missing window.

"I hope your friend can get to my car soon. It won't be safe to drive home with that in place. I won't be able to see out the passenger side at all."

"I'll give him a call in the morning." He tore off a strip of tape. "Let me get your cell phone number so I can call you and let you know what he says."

He applied the tape to the top of the cardboard, and then fitted it over the doorframe while she wrote her phone number on a slip of paper from her purse. She watched him put the final pieces of tape in place, then handed him the paper. Chase pulled out his wallet and slid it inside.

"Are you going to be okay?"

His soft voice sent tears to her eyes. "I'm... I'm a bit rattled." She drew a breath that, to her dismay, shuddered in her chest.

"Are you afraid to be alone?" He stepped closer, forcing her to look up at him. "Because my parents have a guest room. You can go grab your things and I'll take you there right now."

"No, that's okay," she said quickly. No doubt his mother would love that. "I wouldn't want to impose. Besides, I'm not *afraid*. It's just that I'm feeling a bit lonely. I wish my friends had come up with me."

Now why did she tell him that?

"Hey, come here." He pulled her into a gentle hug. "I know you don't know me well, but I'm here. If you feel lonely, you can call me."

For a moment, Caitlin enjoyed the feeling of his strong

arms around her. Her head fit perfectly on his shoulder. Funny, but she'd decided Chase needed a friend not long ago, and it turned out she needed one, too.

"Thanks. I appreciate that a lot." She lifted her head to look up into his eyes. What she saw there set her pulse flittering. She could get totally lost in those eyes. It would be so easy to fall for this guy.

The dateless year made more sense every minute.

She stepped away and folded her arms across her chest. "Uh, I'd better get inside. Thanks." She waved toward the cardboard in her car door. "For that, I mean."

He studied her a moment, then shoved his hands into his pockets. "No problem. So, are we on for dinner tomorrow?"

Oh, how she would love to have dinner with him! But that couldn't be considered anything except a date. And the way her heart was pounding against her rib cage just from looking into his eyes…

She shook her head. "Thanks, but I don't think I can make dinner. I'll probably be helping Nicky get ready."

Questions filled his eyes. She waited for him to ask why she wouldn't go with him to dinner, but after a moment he gave a nod.

"Just the concert, then. I'll pick you up at six forty-five." He turned and walked toward the hotel's side entrance before she could come up with a protest.

Caitlin made sure her car door was locked, dubious though that security measure might be with cardboard in place of glass, then followed him. When she slid her card through the reader, he pulled the door open and held it.

His shoulders looked stiff. Had she offended him? She hadn't intended to. To smooth the awkward moment, she gave a short laugh.

"You know what my first thought was when I saw this stuff

on the floorboard? That I was glad I'd taken my candles into my hotel room when I checked in earlier. I'd hate to lose them."

A low chuckle rumbled in his chest. "Trust me. There's more where those came from."

A thrill zinged through her. Was he saying… *Don't look for hidden meanings.* He probably meant he'd *sell* her all the candles she wanted. Actually, he probably just meant that he runs the factory that makes them. She needed to excuse herself before she said or did anything foolish. She was losing her grip.

She stepped inside. "Good night, Chase. I had a good time. Tell your mom I'm glad she suggested the concert."

"I'll call you in the morning."

He let go of the door, and it whooshed closed with a bang. Caitlin stood staring at the windowless metal, her thoughts whirling. If she'd been on the lookout for a new boyfriend, guys would be avoiding her like she had leprosy. But the minute she decided to guard her heart, up pops Mr. Perfect and practically begs to take her to dinner.

Life just wasn't fair.

As he walked to his pickup, Chase whistled a tuneless version of one of the gospel songs. He'd enjoyed himself tonight, more than he'd expected. Caitlin surprised him at the concert with an enthusiasm that matched Maude's. He'd pegged her as a quiet, sit-in-the-pew-and-listen type. Weren't flute players all into highbrow music? A grin curved his lips at the memory of Caitlin and Maude standing side by side, clapping to the beat of a jazzed-up version of "Power in the Blood." Apparently some flute players appreciated a good country gospel tune.

He rounded the front bumper of the pickup and caught sight of the quick fix he'd performed on her car. A sour ending to an otherwise enjoyable evening.

Of course, she'd gone cold on him when he asked her to dinner. The thought gave him pause as he opened the pickup's door. Weird. She seemed to like him, and yet she didn't want to go out with him. Had he offended her with that hug? She'd looked so vulnerable; it had seemed like a friendly gesture. But it wasn't, not really. She felt good in his arms, like she fit there. And when she'd looked up at him, he'd even wanted to kiss her.

He hadn't felt like kissing a woman in a long time, and when he finally did, she practically ran from him. And yet, unless he was getting his signals completely crossed, she felt at least some of the attraction for him that he felt for her.

Of course, she *had* just discovered that her car had been vandalized. And they'd only met today. Maybe she just needed a little time.

He started the engine and backed out of the parking place. Caitlin had an openness he didn't find in most people. When he looked into her face, he could almost see her thoughts. Like she held nothing back, couldn't if she tried. In her company tonight he'd almost managed to forget the gut-wrenching anxiety of the day.

Almost. But not quite. No wonder she didn't want to go out with him. She'd probably sensed his foul mood all evening. For a few moments at the concert he'd successfully blocked the sight of George Walter Lancaster out of his mind. But when the concert ended, it had come crashing back. The memory haunted him. That, and the sight of all those tinfoil packets in the blue container.

He approached the road leading to the candle factory, and on impulse, he pulled onto it. The building looked dark, deserted. Just behind it and to one side, the glimmer of a light beyond the thick stand of trees bordering the empty parking lot caught his eye. The small trailer where Korey lived sat back from the main road on family property, nearly invisible in daylight. Chase glanced at the illuminated numbers on the dashboard. Just past ten-thirty, still early. He could go home and battle his thoughts, or maybe he could kill an hour or so with his cousin. Korey was always good for a few hours' distraction.

He stopped the truck, backed up on the darkened road, and drove through the factory's parking lot around to the back of the building. Korey's trailer lay at the end of a narrow dirt driveway carved through the trees. The shed he used as a woodworking shop was dark, but a light shone behind the closed miniblinds in the trailer's front window.

Chase parked the truck beside his cousin's car, mounted the rickety metal stairs and knocked on the door.

Korey's voice came from inside. "Who's there?"

"It's the new boss," Chase said, grinning as he used the name Korey teased him with. If all went well, in a couple of years he'd be able to claim that title for real.

From inside came the sound of a scramble. Chase heard a shuffle, a thud and a bang. A minute later, the door jerked open. Korey stood in the doorway, shirtless, barefoot, wearing stained gray sweatpants.

"What are you doing here, dude? It's late."

Chase made a show of looking at his watch. "It's ten-thirty. That's early for you. Don't you usually stay up half the night?" He tilted his head to look behind Korey at the cluttered living room. "Am I interrupting something?"

Korey hesitated. He tossed a quick glance over his shoulder. "No, not a thing." His attitude said something different, but after another pause, he pushed open the door and stepped back. "Come on in."

Chase picked his way around an overflowing laundry basket in the center of the tiny living-room floor, and then hefted a box filled with hardware and woodworking tools from the couch. "Man, you really ought to pick up every now and then."

Korey took the box from Chase's hands and placed it on the corner of a small kitchen table, most of which was taken up by a computer monitor. "Yeah, I know. Mom came by the other day and threatened to torch the place."

Chase sat on the couch, but Korey didn't join him. He stood at the counter, arms crossed, fingers tapping on his skin. Strange behavior for Korey. Normally he didn't mind Chase stopping by to watch a game or something.

"I thought you'd be out in the shop, making a birdhouse." Chase laughed at his own jibe. Korey's love affair with wood began when he was six. He fashioned a lopsided box that went unoccupied by the thousands of birds that inhabited the forest surrounding his parents' house. He couldn't understand why the birds avoided such a terrific place to nest, and his mother hadn't wanted to hurt his tender feelings. Finally, his father took pity on him and pointed out that birds couldn't get inside the house. Since he wasn't allowed to use a power saw, Korey had painted a black circle for the door. Aunt Dot still kept the box hanging from a branch in her backyard.

Korey didn't crack a smile. "Not tonight. I was just…" His gaze slid to the computer on the kitchen table. He gave a shrug. "Surfing."

"Ah."

Chase glanced around the trailer's interior. A typical guy's place. A place where you could prop your feet on the coffee table if you wanted. In a position of honor atop a small television screen stood a large Forbidden Fantasy candle, the only scent Korey had ever created. The TV's screen remained dark. Chase considered suggesting they turn it on and see what was playing on ESPN, but then changed his mind. He wasn't in the mood, and his cousin clearly wasn't, either. He would have liked to tell Korey about his evening with Caitlin, especially their moment in the hotel parking lot. But Korey didn't seem like a receptive audience tonight. He found himself tapping a foot on the floor, much like Korey's finger tapping. An awkward silence pounded against his ears. His normally talkative cousin obviously didn't want to be bothered tonight.

Chase launched himself to his feet. "Okay, well, I guess I'll head on home."

Korey's relief was almost insultingly apparent. His face cleared of the pensive look as he unfolded his arms and crossed to the door in a couple of steps. "All right, dude. See you tomorrow."

The door closed behind Chase before his foot hit the bottom step. He turned and stared at it. Weird. As cousins close to the same age, and with a family that worked together day in and day out, he and Korey had been raised practically as brothers. They'd argued and even occasionally fought, but this was the first time he'd ever felt like Korey didn't want him around. What was up with that?

Caitlin settled the blanket over her legs, leaned back against two fluffy pillows, and dialed Liz's number on her cell phone. Her friend picked up on the second ring.

"Hey, girl! How you doing up there in Hoosier land?"

She smiled at the energy in Liz's voice. Love had definitely brightened the attitude of the previously surly cello player.

"Great. But can you hold on a sec? I want to three-way Jazzy."

"Uh-oh." Liz became suspicious. "What's happening up there? It's either really good or really bad if the situation calls for a three-way call."

Caitlin laughed. "Just hold on."

She pressed the hold button on her phone, dialed Jazzy's number and then pressed Link to connect the call.

Jazzy answered without unnecessary greetings. "It's about time you called. I expected you to let me know when you got there safely."

Liz's low laugh sounded through the line. "What are you, her mommy?"

"Liz?" Surprise colored Jazzy's tone. "Where are you?"

"She's at home, and I'm in Indiana," Caitlin explained. "Since you're both supposed to be here in this hotel room with me, I figured we'd do the next best thing and have a virtual pajama party via cell phone."

"Good idea," Jazzy said. "I'll make the popcorn. Y'all want butter?"

"Funny girl," Liz commented dryly. "Cate, how's the room?"

Caitlin glanced at her surroundings. "Typical hotel room. A dresser, television, a minibar that I haven't opened yet. Two double beds. A sign on the front desk said we get free wireless, so if you bring your laptop you can check your e-mail."

"Good." Liz's fiancé lived in Park City, Utah, so telephones and e-mail were their primary methods of communication.

"But is it clean?" Jazzy, the ever-cautious clean freak, asked.

Caitlin could still smell the comforting odor of the house-keeper's cleaning solution. "Even clean enough for you," she assured Jazzy.

"I'm still bringing Lysol."

Caitlin laughed. "Of course you are."

"So, have you found anything really good in all those shops?" Jazzy asked. "Like, maybe, wedding presents for your two best friends?"

"Not yet, but I'm going to do some serious shopping

tomorrow." Caitlin sobered. "Listen, the reason I called this pajama party is because I need your advice. Something's going on up here."

"Let me guess," Liz said. "You met a guy."

An image of Chase loomed in Caitlin's mind. "Yes, but there's a couple of complications." She explained her decision about the dateless year, and then brought them up to date on meeting Chase and his mother, and their evening at the church.

Liz's voice was serious. "I think you're wise to hold off on dating for a while. You're still hurting from Glenn."

"The jerk," Jazzy put in.

Caitlin smiled at the loyalty in her voice. "Chase lost his best friend a year ago, and I don't think he's opened up to anyone since. Tonight he seemed to want to talk to me about it. I think he needs a friend more than anything."

"I'm hearing something in your voice when you mention this guy. Are you sure all you're interested in offering him is friendship?" Liz asked.

Caitlin plucked at a piece of fuzz on the blanket. Trust Liz to see to the heart of the matter. "He *is* very attractive. In fact, if I hadn't come to my decision just a few hours before I met him, I'd be falling for him hard."

"Well," Jazzy said, "you take care of yourself first. Let him find a friend somewhere else. Or let his mother find him one."

Caitlin laughed. Then she remembered the end to the evening. She gave them the bad news. "One other thing happened. When he brought me back to the hotel, we discovered someone had broken my car window."

"What?" Alarm made Jazzy's voice tight. "Is the hotel not safe?"

"It's as safe as any, I guess. It was probably my own fault," she admitted. "I shouldn't have left my shopping bags in plain sight on the seat."

Liz spoke up. "Well, as long as nobody's been killed there, we're okay."

In the past two years the trio had taken only two road trips to play at out-of-town weddings. Both times they had been unwillingly entangled in a murder case. And both times, one of them had narrowly escaped with their lives.

Caitlin smoothed the blanket with a flat hand. She should tell Jazzy and Liz about the body in the park, and about Chase's involvement. But she knew what they'd say. They'd insist she return home immediately. And if she refused, they'd come up here and forcibly drag her home. Forget their commitment to play at the wedding this weekend, they'd say no wedding was worth it. And they just might be right.

But now that she was up here, she couldn't leave. How awful would it be to ditch a bride mere days before her wedding? What would the poor girl do for music?

Besides, Chase's involvement in this latest murder was purely accidental. And he'd been nothing but kind to her. The least she could do was provide a friendly ear and a reason to forget the painful memories of his friend's death.

At least the body wasn't found in the hotel.

Caitlin chose her words carefully. "Nobody's been killed in this hotel. Don't worry. We're perfectly safe on this trip."

TEN

"So, how was the hot date last night?"

Chase ignored Alex's smirk as he unlocked the door to the factory at seven o'clock Thursday morning. Was that a touch of jealousy he detected in the lothario's voice? The guy wasn't accustomed to watching someone else score with the ladies while he was left on the sidelines. Apparently he didn't like it much.

"We had a great time." He pulled the door open and held it for Alex to step inside. As he passed, Chase couldn't help adding, "We're going out again tonight." Not to dinner, as he'd hoped, but Alex didn't need to know that.

"You had a great time *at church?*" From his tone, Alex didn't believe anyone could have a good time at church.

"Absolutely. The whole place was rocking." Chase grinned at Alex's incredulous stare. "Next time we have a gospel group visit, you're welcome to come with me and see for yourself."

He snorted and stepped past Chase, toward the workroom, mumbling something about cold days. Chuckling, Chase headed for the office.

Before he'd even taken his seat, Korey followed him in. "Hey, dude."

Chase started to bid his cousin good morning, but stopped

as he got a good look at him. Korey looked terrible. Pouches of dark skin sagged beneath red-rimmed eyes. He hadn't bothered to comb his hair, and though he had thrown on a wrinkled T-shirt and flip-flops, he wore the same stained sweats from last night. He'd looked tired and distracted last night, but not like this.

"What happened to you?" Chase asked, alarmed at the overnight change in his cousin. "Are you sick or something?"

Korey dropped into the chair at the second desk and leaned his head against the back, eyes closed. "That's what I came to tell you. I've been up all night, didn't get any sleep, and I feel lousy. I'm not working today, okay?"

Chase nodded. "No problem. Stay home and rest. You didn't have to come over. You could have called."

Korey lifted his shoulders. "I saw your truck pull into the parking lot and figured I'd come tell you." He cracked an eye open. "Don't tell my mom, okay? She'll want to bring me chicken soup or something, and then she'll stick around to 'take care of me.' I can't handle that today."

He looked like he could use some taking care of, but Chase completely understood not wanting your mother hovering over you.

"Are you sure you don't need to see a doctor?" Chase eyed him with concern. "You look awful. I mean, really bad."

He gave a sardonic snort. "Thanks, dude." He hefted himself out of the chair and stumbled toward the door. "Nah, don't need a doctor. A few hours of sleep and I'll be fine."

Chase wasn't so sure, but other than hog-tie the guy and drag him to the doctor's office, he couldn't do anything. "Okay, if you say so. Don't worry about anything here. We'll handle it."

After Korey left, Chase shook his head as he slid into his seat. Korey spent so much time away from the factory, his absence today probably wouldn't even be noticed. His focus lately was on woodworking, and making enough products to open his own shop downtown in a couple of years with the money Chase paid him for his share in Good Things In Wax. That goal had taken him away from the day-to-day operation of the candle factory for months.

Most of Chase's daily conversations with the Lord took place at night as he lay in bed waiting for sleep, a result of the childhood habit of bedtime prayers. But today, as he sat at his desk first thing in the morning, he found himself mouthing a prayer for his cousin's health.

"The candle wasn't in her car."

Beads of sweat broke out on Ed's forehead. His grip on the telephone tightened so that the instrument shook against his ear. The walls of the candle-shop office seemed to move toward him, box him in. He closed his eyes.

"This is a disaster." His voice shook, but he didn't care. "You've got to take care of this."

"I know! I'm trying. She must have taken it inside with her."

Ed sank against the edge of the desk. "You don't think she burned it, do you?"

"Well, have the cops showed up at your store yet?"

Panic threatened to close his throat. That's exactly what they'd do. They'd come in here with a warrant, search the place and cart him off in handcuffs in front of his employees and the whole town. But he wouldn't go down by himself. "They'll go to the candle factory, too. We're both in up to our necks if we don't get that candle back. You're going to have to search her hotel room. I know she's going to be out this afternoon. She'll be at the middle school giving my kid a flute lesson. Get into her room then."

"I don't know which room is hers, and even if I did, how would I get inside?"

Ed jerked to his feet. "I don't care how you do it, just do it." He glanced quickly at the door and lowered his voice. "Look, whatever you have to do, do it quickly."

A pause. "You mean that?"

The sweat on Ed's forehead grew cold. Two people had died at this man's hands already. When Ed first agreed to this crazy scheme, he'd never anticipated things going this far. He was going to make a ton of money, that's all. Pay off the store and the mortgage on his home. Pad the kids' college funds.

He'd never realized he was entering into partnership with a cold-blooded killer. And a moron, besides.

"I don't want to know anymore." His voice rasped, his throat raw. "Just get that candle back."

A grunt sounded in his ear as he disconnected the call. He stood still, paralyzed by indecision. What should he do? Sit around and wait for the cops to show up? That would drive him crazy. Every time a customer came through the door, he'd think the cops were coming for him.

His gaze fell on the locked storage cabinet where he kept the special candles. One thing was for sure, he had to get them out of here. If the police searched the store, he'd make sure they came up empty-handed. But where could he put them so they wouldn't be found?

ELEVEN

"I really appreciate you leaving work to run me around." Caitlin took Chase's proffered hand as she stepped up into his truck outside the repair shop. "I feel bad for taking you away from the factory."

"Don't worry about it. Our delivery guy didn't show up for work today, so I've been out and about this morning anyway." His voice lowered. "Besides, driving you around is my pleasure."

His grin held an intimate quality that brought an answering flush to warm her cheeks. She refused to let her hand linger in his after she was seated. Pulling it away, she clasped it in her other one. When he closed the door, she leaned back in the sun-warmed cab. A few seconds to catch her breath while he circled the truck to the driver's side.

Good grief! My heart is fluttering like a lovesick teenager. Back in high school, she'd mooned over a football player who turned his nose up at her hero worship. Mom's heart-to-heart explained that boys didn't like girls who were so obvious with their emotions. "Play hard to get," she advised. "Let them feel like they've won a prize when they finally get your attention. Because, sweetie, they have!"

Apparently, Mom was right. Here she was, not *playing*

hard to get, but trying for real to make sure she wasn't sending out vibes. And what happens? First the guy gives her a hug that almost sends her into cardiac arrest, and then he tells her he likes driving her around. Sheesh! If she'd been flirting with him, wanting his attention, he'd probably be heading for the next county, to hide out until she left town. Figures.

She shouldn't have accepted his offer to give her a ride after dropping her car off at the repair shop. But when he'd called this morning and told her his friend would fix it, he'd practically insisted. What could she do?

He opened the door and slid inside. "I'm just sorry my buddy can't get your car back to you until this afternoon."

The truck pulled away from Caitlin's car, waiting in a line outside the garage doors. "I'm grateful they can fix it today. I was afraid I'd have to wait until I got home."

"What time are you supposed to be at the middle school?"

"Three-thirty." Caitlin glanced at the clock. Just after ten. Hours to kill before the time she'd arranged to meet Nicky. "You can just go ahead and drop me off in town. I'll wander around, do some shopping, then get a taxi to the school this afternoon."

"If you want." He drove with one hand at the top of the steering wheel, his posture relaxed. "But I'm kind of in the mood for a cup of coffee. There's an ice-cream parlor with great hazelnut coffee downtown, if you're interested."

Uh-oh. Skating close to *date* territory. *Lord, why couldn't this bride have decided to get married* next *year? Like, three hundred and sixty-four days from now?*

She turned a tight smile in his direction. "I'd better not."

Chase gave her a sideways look, then drove in silence. Caitlin's shoulders sagged. She hadn't meant to offend him, but apparently she'd done just that. While she struggled for something to say, he pulled into a small parking lot.

He shoved the gearshift lever into park and turned in the seat to face her. "Can I ask you a question?"

She swallowed. "Sure."

"Why don't you want to go out with me?" He held up a hand to stop her from answering quickly. "Not that I'm saying I'm all that great or anything, but you seemed like you had a good time at my church last night. And you didn't seem to mind me pushing my way into your concert tonight. Yet you won't let me take you to dinner, or even buy you a cup of coffee." He paused as he looked at her carefully. "My mother scared you off, didn't she?"

Caitlin laughed. "I think your mother is charming." Then she bit her lip. "It's not that I don't want to go out with you. I just can't."

"Do you have a boyfriend?"

"No." How to put this without sounding like a complete fool? "Well, I did, but he broke up with me a month ago and started dating a woman he works with."

He winced. "Ouch."

She straightened a twist in her seat belt. "I've had a pretty rough time. And actually, on the drive up here, I came to a decision." She told him about the dateless year.

Chase gave her his full attention, and when she was finished, he nodded slowly. "I think that's wise. After Kevin died last year, I broke up with my girlfriend. I just lost interest in the relationship. She started going out with another guy the next week, and they got married three months later." He shook his head. "I've worried she was on the rebound. I hope she didn't make a mistake because I hurt her."

Caitlin saw guilt in his slumped shoulders. "You can't blame yourself." She covered his hand with hers. The contact sent warmth through her core, reminding her of the feel of his arms around her, and she quickly pulled away. He didn't seem to notice, thank goodness.

"I'm glad we've cleared the air." She unsnapped her seatbelt. "Because I'd love a cup of coffee. As friends." She smiled. "Dutch treat."

"Sounds good." He opened the door and started to get out, then turned a grin her way. "Uh, I'll let you open your own door, friend."

A crowd filled the busy shop, an old-fashioned ice-cream parlor complete with vinyl-covered stools at the polished counter and paddle fans circling overhead. They stood in line to place their orders while the scent of warm waffle cones filled the shop. Round tubs of ice cream lined the inside of the glass-topped freezer to the left of the cash register. She opened her mouth to tell the cashier she wanted a cup of coffee, and caved to temptation.

"I'll have a scoop of Rocky Road and a cup of hazelnut coffee."

Chase's eyebrows arched. "Ice cream at ten in the morning?"

She grinned at him. "I'm on vacation."

"Well, then, I can't let my new friend indulge alone, can I?"

Chase grabbed a table in the corner when a couple vacated it, and they slid onto wrought iron chairs. On the other side of the window, people filed by on the charming streets of Little Nashville.

"They say you can tell a lot about a person by their ice-cream choices." A grin hovered at the corners of Chase's lips as he eyed her dish of Rocky Road.

"Really?" Caitlin inspected a loaded spoon. "What does this say about me? That I'm soft, like a marshmallow?"

"Possibly." His head cocked sideways. "Or maybe you're nutty."

She drew herself up in mock indignation. "Hey! I've been insulted."

He laughed. "Okay, seriously." He drew his eyebrows together in solemn contemplation of her ice-cream dish. "Rocky Road is a blend of flavors, which says you're not satisfied with anything plain. I think it means you have a wide range of interests and enjoy variety in life." He sat back with a wide smile. "How'd I do?"

"Hmmm. Good comeback." She allowed her ruffled feathers to smooth as she took another bite. "What about you, Mr. Ice-Cream Analyst? What does Double Chocolate Chunk say about you?"

He lifted his sugar cone. "That I'm chunky?"

Hardly that. Caitlin's glance skimmed over his muscled arms, strong shoulders and what she could see of the trim waist. A blush threatened, and she combated it with a quick response.

"That's too easy. Come on, a double dose of chocolate has to say something about your personality." She leaned against the heart-shaped chair back and tapped her spoon on her lips as she thought. "I know. You work twice as hard as anyone else, not because you have to but because you enjoy the results. You're not satisfied by simply getting a job done, but are driven to do it exceptionally well. In other words, you're an overachiever."

His smile broke free. "Very good. And not far off the mark, either. I've been known to display workaholic tendencies, or so my mother tells me."

"And yet, here you are." Caitlin swept the room with her spoon. "In the middle of the morning, and not at work."

"Hey, a guy's allowed time off for good behavior every now and then." He propped his elbows on the table, the cone held in both hands.

"True." Caitlin scooped up another spoonful. "So tell me about the factory. You mentioned yesterday it's a family business."

He nodded. "My grandfather started making candles when he was a teenager, and opened the business when he was in his twenties."

"Does he still work there?"

"No, he died three years ago. Heart attack." He heaved a sigh. "He was a workaholic, too, which I've tried to keep in mind. Anyway, in his will he divided the company into fourths."

"Fourths?"

"My mom, my aunt, my cousin and I all own equal shares." He used a finger to catch a drip of chocolate before it ran down the side of his cone. "But in another year or two I'm going to buy out their interests."

"They don't like making candles?"

His shoulders heaved with a laugh. "My cousin hates the family business. But he's a talented woodworker, so he hopes to open a store selling handmade furniture and other woodcrafts. Mom and Aunt Dot enjoy the work, but they're both nearing retirement age. Dad retired last year, and Mom is ready to hand over the business so the two of them can start traveling."

The hint of passion glimmering in his eyes gave them depth. Caitlin took a guess at the reason. "You have plans for the factory when you own it."

His eyes gleamed as he nodded. "My degree is in procedural engineering. I can see so many ways to streamline our processes to increase our production levels. And our equipment needs updating as well. When Grandpa was alive he wouldn't even consider my suggestions." He straightened in his chair and assumed a scowl. "'I'm not wasting money on any of those newfangled ideas, boy. I've been making candles longer than you've been alive.'"

Caitlin laughed at his imitation of a crotchety old man. "He sounds like a character."

"Oh, he was." Chase sobered. "Don't get me wrong. I don't mean to disrespect him. He was a talented candle maker, and I learned everything I know about the business from him. But he was not a risk taker. Whereas *I* can see the possibilities, and I'm not afraid to try something new."

Determination showed in the firm set of his jaw. Caitlin had no trouble believing he would succeed in his plans. She scraped the last bite of ice cream from her dish as he bit into his crunchy cone.

"What about you?" he asked. "Do you have aspirations to play your flute with the London Symphony Orchestra?" A playful grin flashed onto his face. "Or maybe a country gospel band?"

She acknowledged the reference with a crooked smile. The short answer to his question was no, but then he'd want to know her plans. Becoming a wife and mother didn't sound like a very lofty goal compared to reengineering a factory. And it was entirely at odds with her recent decision to wait a year before dating. But truly, that's what she'd wanted from the first moment she cradled a baby doll in her arms.

"Oh, I don't know." She kept her gaze fixed on his disappearing ice-cream cone. "I enjoy performing at weddings with my friends, but a professional orchestra?" She shook her head. "It's never been one of my dreams."

"You like working with kids." He peeled the paper off the bottom of his cone. "At least you seem to, since you're spending your time off helping a kid do well in that concert tonight."

"I do enjoy working with young people, especially if they have talent and a desire to learn, like Nicky Graham." She folded her forearms on the table and leaned forward. "I love helping them realize what they can accomplish and watching them succeed. It's satisfying, somehow, to know I helped them realize their potential."

His head rose and dipped in a slow nod. "You're a nurturer."

She gave a startled laugh. "I suppose I am. Doesn't sound very exciting, does it?"

His voice became a low rumble. "I think it's admirable. You have to care about people to want to nurture them. Not many do."

The full-fledged compliment left Caitlin fumbling for a response. She couldn't hold his gaze.

"Here," she said. "You've got chocolate on your chin."

Without thinking, she reached across the table and touched his face with her napkin. He held her gaze as she dabbed at the drop. When her finger brushed his lip, warmth spread through her insides.

"Thank you." His soft tone sent a ripple after the warmth.

Caitlin jerked her hand back and dropped it into her lap. *Okay, there's one to remember: next time, my new friend had better wipe his own face.*

When they stepped outside, Chase heard a familiar voice calling his name. "Chase Hollister!"

Caitlin glanced over his shoulder. Her face lit up. "It's Mrs. Jackson from your church."

He turned in time to see Maude hurry across the street, a wide smile on her face.

Great. My mother will hear about this before I can get back to the factory.

"Well, look at the two of you, out together in the middle of the day." Maude's gaze slid from him to Caitlin. "And did I see you coming out of the ice-cream parlor?"

"Hello, Mrs. Jackson," Caitlin said. "Yes, we stopped in for a treat."

The woman took Caitlin's hand in both of hers. "Call me Maude, honey. Everybody does. Even my grandchildren call me Granny Maude." She beamed in Chase's direction. "It does my tired old eyes good to see you two young people together." A dimple in her cheek deepened. *"Again."*

Judging by the glee on the woman's face, Mom wasn't the only one who would hear about Chase Hollister's second date with the blond out-of-towner. After a glance at Caitlin's suddenly red face, Chase shoved his hands in his pockets and studied a miniscule chip in the paint on the ice-cream shop's doorjamb.

"I had to take my car to have some work done," Caitlin explained, "and Chase was kind enough to give me a ride."

"There's nobody nicer than our Chase, and that's God's own truth. He's a true gentleman, through and through."

Chase bit back a groan. Terrific. Now Maude was extolling his virtues. This was starting to look like a full-fledged frontal attack of the Blue Hills Matchmaking Society. He needed to get out of here quickly, and he couldn't leave Caitlin in the woman's clutches.

He put a hand under Caitlin's arm and tugged gently in an attempt to pry her away from Maude's grip. "It's great to see you, Maude. We have to be going. I've got to get back to work."

Maude held on tight. "Work? Why, Chase Hollister, just look at that sky." Chase examined the bright blue expanse, as instructed. "Have you ever seen a prettier day? You and this fine young lady should enjoy the weather. Go for a walk in the park." She added temptingly, "The flowers are in full bloom."

"Thanks for the tip." Chase tugged at Caitlin again, harder this time, and Maude finally let go. "We'll keep it in mind."

"All right. Well, good-bye, honey." She took a step back and wiggled her fingers at Caitlin. "Hope to see you again real soon."

As they walked away, Caitlin giggled. "Looks like all the older women in your life are eager to find you a girlfriend."

Chase groaned. "I put up with it all the time from my mom and Aunt Dot. But I never expected they'd recruit the women from church."

At least Caitlin was laughing about the incident. Given her determination *not* to enter into a relationship for a year, Maude's attention could have scared her off for good.

They walked down the sidewalk easily, their strides matching. How refreshing to find a woman who wasn't desperate to get a ring on her finger. He'd found himself relaxing as they talked over ice cream, glad to see that their hug last night hadn't made things awkward between them. But he couldn't seem to get it out of his mind. The way she'd felt in his arms... Well, he had to respect her decision not to date. Even if he didn't really want to.

Maude's suggestion sounded like a good one, though. Not the part about walking in the park—he shuddered at the thought. But the sky was clear, the temperature pleasant, and Caitlin's company soothed his jangled nerves. Spending a few hours with her sounded a lot more appealing than the Freesia and Orange Blossom pours on the schedule for today. Alex and Irene could handle those with no problem, and Mom and Aunt Dot could hold down the fort in the front for a few hours.

As he searched for a way to casually suggest that he accompany her on her shopping expedition, they approached Buckeye Street.

"Hey, one of my employees, Willie, lives down this street." He glanced to the left. "Only a couple of blocks that way. Would you mind if we ran down there?"

Caitlin's brow creased. "Why?"

"Because he didn't show up for work this morning. I tried to call a couple of times, but couldn't get an answer. It'll only take a minute to check on him."

She considered for a moment, then her brow cleared. "Okay. I'm not in any hurry."

They turned down the street and walked the three blocks in companionable silence.

"There it is." Chase pointed out an older frame house with a rickety white railing around a deep, covered porch. "He rents an apartment in the basement."

Caitlin came to a halt on the sidewalk, staring intently. Chase followed her gaze, and saw Willie's beat-up old van parked at the curb.

"Something wrong?" he asked.

For a moment she didn't reply. "N-no. It's just that…" She gave her head a quick shake. "Oh, nothing."

Chase watched her for a moment, then let it go. He led her down the driveway past a half dozen trash bags piled against the peeling wood siding, their tops gaping open. The smell of garbage rotting in the hot sun made his nose curl. Chase's shoes crunched on chunks of broken concrete as he descended five crumbling steps to the basement. He knocked on the door.

Nothing.

Exchanging a glance with Caitlin, who waited in the grass, he pounded with a fist. "Willie? Hey, Willie, are you in there?"

Not a sound from inside. To Chase's right, another door opened, this one leading into the main floor of the house. An elderly woman in a housecoat stepped out holding a scruffy dog.

"He ain't answering." Her gravelly voice gave testimony to years of smoking. "I been trying to wake him all morning, since I seen his van out front." She peered first at Caitlin, and then at Chase. "You friends of Mr. Evans'?"

"I'm his employer."

"From out at the candle factory?"

When Chase nodded, the old lady made her way to the top

of the basement steps. Pink scalp showed through her thin gray hair, and the threadbare housecoat she wore could have used a good washing. Spindly legs extended below an uneven hemline, and her feet were covered by worn slippers.

"I'm a mite worried about him. He was actin' strange when he came home last night. Jumpy."

Willie *always* acted jumpy, but Chase didn't mention that.

Concern flooded Caitlin's features. "Maybe he's ill and can't come to the door."

The woman turned to her, nodding. "I thought so, too, but I hated to go in there with no cause." Her glance slid back to Chase. "But you're his boss." She fished in a deep pocket of the housecoat and pulled out a simple metal ring with a single key, which she thrust toward Chase. "Here. You open it."

Indecision warred in Chase. What if Willie was just sleeping off a hangover or something? That would be completely in character. On the other hand, Willie never missed work. He'd showed up a few times when he shouldn't have, still not quite sobered up from the night before. Chase had been forced to send him home, but at least he always showed up.

"I think you should, Chase." Caitlin wrapped her arms around her middle and nodded toward the door. "He might need help in there."

She was right. Chase climbed halfway up the stairs, took the key from the landlady's hand and returned to the bottom. He pounded on the door once again.

"Willie, if you're in there, say something." No response. Chase fit the key into the lock. "I'm coming in."

He unlocked the door and turned the handle. The air inside had the cool, dank feel of basements everywhere. A smell struck him, a blend of the familiar and the unfamiliar. Chase stepped inside.

And froze.

A slightly built man lay face down on a large throw rug in front of a threadbare sofa, his head at an unnatural sideways angle. Willie. An incredible amount of blood soaked the thin rug. Chase's stomach lurched. He kept his ice cream down through sheer willpower. From his vantage point, he could see that Willie's throat had been cut.

Just like the man in the park. Just like Kevin.

He backed out, and pulled the door closed. He couldn't look at the two women standing at the top of the stairs. Instead, he rested his forehead against the door.

"Chase?" Caitlin sounded worried. "Is everything okay?"

Chase swallowed. Hard. "We'd better call 911. Willie's dead."

TWELVE

Caitlin stood beside Mrs. Poulson, the owner of the house, and watched a line of deputies march down to the basement. At the top of the stairs, Chase looked faintly green as he spoke with a detective. No wonder. She'd be a basket case after finding two dead bodies in as many days.

Mrs. Poulson's voice shook as she spoke. "I should have known. My Bo-Bo here, he just kept barking and barking. He musta heard something." A choked sob stilled her voice. The wiry-haired dog in her arms extended its neck to lick her chin with a pink tongue.

"I'm so sorry." Caitlin put an arm around her thin shoulders and squeezed.

Chase and the detective approached.

"Mrs. Poulson," Chase said, "this is Detective Jenkins of the Brown County Sheriff's Department. He'd like to ask you a few questions."

"I didn't hear nothing," she said immediately, "but my Bo-Bo woke me up in the night barking. I think he musta been protecting me."

The detective reached out to pet Bo-Bo, but pulled his hand quickly away when the creature growled at him. He cleared his throat. "What time was that, ma'am?"

"Around one, I think."

"Could you tell me about the victim, Mr.—" He tossed a questioning look at Chase.

"Evans," Chase supplied. "Willie Evans."

Jenkins smiled at Mrs. Poulson. "What can you tell me about Mr. Evans, ma'am?"

The old woman shook her head. "He never caused no trouble. Kept to himself mostly. Didn't have visitors. Quiet. Paid his rent on time. He was a good renter." The dog squirmed in her arms, and she held him tight.

"How long has he rented from you?"

"'Bout six months, I guess. Ever since he started working over at that candle factory. Mr. Evans delivers—" Her throat moved as she swallowed. "He *delivered* their candles for them."

Caitlin squeezed the woman's shoulders again.

A deputy approached. He cast a furtive glance at Chase, then said, "Detective, c'mere and look at what I found."

Detective Jenkins turned to follow the man around the corner of the house. After exchanging a glance with Caitlin, Chase followed. Her heart wrenched to see the droop of his shoulders. Poor Chase. She fought the impulse to run after him and slip a comforting arm around him, but the memory of their hug last night—and the torrent of feelings it caused—stopped her. She'd better keep her distance, physically. But he needed a friend with him right now. With a final smile for Mrs. Poulson, she trailed behind the men.

The deputy stopped at the pile of black plastic trash bags and pointed. "Look there."

One of the bags lay on its side, and the garbage had partially spilled out. Caitlin saw immediately what had caught the deputy's attention. Half-buried beneath a pile of slimy black banana peels and wadded up tissues lay a glass jar. No mistaking that kind of jar.

A candle.

She sucked in a breath. A dark purple Forbidden Fantasy candle.

Her whirling thoughts were interrupted by the arrival of a girl trotting up the driveway beside the police cruisers, a camera hanging from a strap around her neck and a bulky bag swinging at her side.

"Sorry I'm late, fellas." The girl flashed an apologetic smile around. "I was taking an early lunch. I'll get started working the scene immediately. Just point me in the right direction."

Detective Jenkins stabbed a finger toward the candle. "Get pictures of this. And somebody give me some gloves."

Chase disconnected his call and went to stand near Caitlin, to watch the deputies dig through the garbage.

"How'd your mom take the news?" she asked.

Chase shook his head. "I didn't tell her about Willie. News like that shouldn't be delivered on the phone."

Caitlin, arms wrapped around her middle, hugged herself as she nodded. "I'm so sorry you're going through this, Chase."

He heard concern in her voice. Having her calming presence nearby made the gruesome discovery of Willie's body a little more tolerable. He gave her a grateful smile. "Thanks."

Detective Jenkins broke away from the others and came toward him. His stern expression caused Chase's muscles to tense. He was about to be put through the wringer, and from personal experience, he knew Jenkins was an expert at cranking the handle. Chase forced himself to relax. He had done nothing wrong.

Jenkins wasted no breath on preamble. "I don't know how you're involved, Hollister, but you are."

Frustration churned in Chase's stomach. Frustration—and a touch of fear. Willie was the second person close to him who'd been murdered within a year.

What's going on around here?

He did his best to keep his expression impassive as he faced the detective. "I know it looks that way, but I promise you, I'm not. It's just a coincidence."

"I don't believe in coincidences."

Chase bristled at the man's flat tone. Was Jenkins calling him a liar? "I don't care what you believe, Detective. I'm telling you the truth. There's no connection between Willie and Kevin Duncan. They never even met, as far as I know. Kevin died a year ago, and Willie has only been at the factory for—"

He snapped his mouth shut. When had Willie joined the Good Things In Wax team? Korey brought him on board right about the time they'd signed the contract with the Candle Corner, which was about six months ago. No connection to Kevin at all. But to his cousin…

"Yes?" Detective Jenkins's eyebrows formed arches as he waited for Chase to continue.

Chase tried to wet his lips with a dry tongue. He looked at Caitlin, whose sympathetic smile encouraged him to continue. "We hired Willie a few months after Kevin was killed."

"I see. What do you know about Evans? Did you run a background check before you put him on the payroll?"

"We checked his driving record, and made sure he had the proper ID, a social security card and all that. Since we were hiring him as a deliveryman, that's all we were concerned with."

"Did he fill out paperwork? An application, I-9, all that?"

Chase ground some grass beneath his heel. Did he think they were complete idiots when it came to hiring an employee? "Of course he did. We're running a business. We follow all the rules, Detective."

A cold smile flashed on the detective's face for a second. "I'm sure you do. I'll need to see any documents you have on record for him."

Chase nearly said something about needing a warrant, but he decided against it. Willie might not have been his favorite person, but the man was dead. Anything he could do to help the police apprehend his killer, he should do. "No problem. Can we go now?"

He put an arm under Caitlin's elbow and made as if to step away, but Jenkins's reply stopped him.

"Not quite." He looked toward the group of deputies and shouted, "Matthews, bring that bag over here, please!"

Matthews approached carrying a large, clear zipper bag. As he neared, Chase got a good look at the contents. His stomach dropped to his feet.

Not one, but *three* Forbidden Fantasy candles.

Jenkins's gaze remained locked on to Chase's face as he held out a hand, and Matthews slapped a pair of rubber gloves into his palm. "They have a rather distinctive odor. Hard to miss. Smells like black jelly beans and something else."

"Eucalyptus," Caitlin put in.

Jenkins looked at her for a moment, then nodded. "That's it. George Lancaster's apartment reeked of it."

Ah. That explained the detective's obscure comment about jelly beans yesterday.

As he talked, he pulled on the gloves, opened the bag and withdrew one of jars. When he twisted off the lid, the blended aroma of eucalyptus and licorice filled the windless air around them.

"I couldn't help but notice that your company manufactures this candle, Hollister. The same company that employed our latest murder victim. And the first murder victim, who was also your friend." He kept his gaze fixed on Chase as he turned the candle absently in his hand. Then he looked at Caitlin. "And last night, your car was broken into while you were in his company. I ran a background check on you this morning."

Caitlin stiffened with outrage. Her mouth opened to say something, but Jenkins cut her off.

"Standard procedure, I assure you. I found nothing. Not even a parking ticket. But then today you turn up in his company again, along with yet another murder victim." His gaze slid back to pierce Chase. "Now, tell me again how you're not involved."

Cotton filled Chase's mouth as he stared at the candle. "I…" He swallowed and tried again. "I don't know what to say."

Thoughts whirled in his brain. Forbidden Fantasy was Korey's creation. Korey had hired Willie. And lately Korey had been acting… well, odd. More distracted than usual.

No! He's my cousin. Korey's a good guy.

Of course Chase had thought Kevin was a good guy, too.

He ran a hand across his forehead, trying to focus his thoughts.

"No wick," Caitlin said. Chase and Jenkins both looked at her. "There's no wick in this candle."

Jenkins straightened. "It's been melted?"

Excitement made Caitlin's nod quick. "I use a candle warmer to melt candles instead of burn them. The wick always slips down into the hot wax."

Jenkins stared at the candle. His eyes widened.

Chase nodded. "There's something inside the candles." *Korey, no! What have you done?*

The detective's jaw hardened. "And I'll bet I know what it is, too." The detective extended the jar in his gloved hand. "Do you have any more of these?"

Chase wiped his sweating palms on his jeans. "We manufacture them exclusively for Ed Graham at the Candle Corner downtown. That's the only place they're sold. In fact, Willie delivered a shipment there yesterday."

Jenkins's gaze snapped to the deputy's face. "I want a warrant to search that store and every piece of property Graham owns."

The deputy whirled toward the line of cruisers in front of the house. "I'm on it."

Chase couldn't think. This could not be happening. His own cousin, involved in a drug ring right under his nose? Using the family business, no less? But the pieces fit.

Lord, I've got to be the worst judge of character on the face of the earth.

Still, he couldn't bring himself to point the finger at his cousin in front of Detective Jenkins. Not yet. Not until he'd confronted Korey himself. Let the police get their warrant, search Ed Graham's store and find whatever was hidden in those candles themselves.

Korey was at home in bed today. Was he really sick? Chase's hands tightened into fists. Just wait until he got hold of his cousin.

Caitlin climbed up into Chase's pickup and pulled the door closed behind her. She glanced at her watch. Two-forty. That police detective had kept them there for hours, asking the same questions over and over.

On the other side of the truck's cab, Chase slid behind the wheel. "Are you hungry? We could grab something before I take you to the school."

The morning's ice cream had long since worn off, but Caitlin couldn't eat. Her thoughts kept circling around Nicky and how devastated she would be when she discovered her father was selling drugs. And Janie, too. Because Caitlin was convinced neither of them had any idea.

She wrinkled her nose. "I'm not very hungry." The pickup

maneuvered out of the parking lot. She turned in her seat to face him. "Oh, Chase, how will I act normal around Nicky and Janie, knowing the police are searching their house the whole time we're practicing?"

"Would you rather not go?" He took his foot off the gas pedal, and the truck slowed. "I'll take you back to your hotel if you prefer."

An image of Nicky's anxious face loomed in her mind. "No, I'd better go. But how long do you think it will be before the police get their warrant?"

"I don't know. Not much longer, I'd guess." His lips tightened into a firm line. "I just hope they find that shipment of candles we delivered there yesterday, so they can nail that guy."

"They will. There were a bunch of candles in those boxes I saw. Mr. Graham couldn't have sold the whole shipment in one night."

Chase went still. His head turned toward her, eyes wide. "A whole shipment—minus one."

Caitlin gasped. "The candle you gave me."

He held her gaze as he nodded. "It's still on the shelf under the cash register. And we don't need a warrant to look inside that one."

Caitlin glanced at her watch. She still had thirty-five minutes before she had to be at the school. "Let's go."

The bell over the door sounded, and true to his prediction, the knot in Ed's insides jangled in unison with his nerves. He raised his head from restocking the potpourri bags, certain this time he'd see the gray uniform of a police officer in the doorway. Instead, a trio of smiling tourists filed inside, chattering as they entered. Breath flooded his lungs as a band around his chest loosened.

He put on his professional face. "Good afternoon, ladies."

"Hello," they sang in unison.

The telephone rang. Ed glanced toward the sales counter, where Laura reached for the receiver. His smile broadened for his customers. "Are you just browsing, or can I help you find something in particular?"

"Oh, we're just browsing at the moment." The first woman reached for a decorative candle as her friends moved down the center aisle, whispering to each other.

Ed kept his expression pleasant as he nodded. "Well, if you have any questions, just let me know."

"Uh, Ed?"

Ed turned away from the customer. When he caught sight of Laura's face, the invisible band once again squeezed the breath out of his lungs. She held the receiver in a loose grip, her eyes round with alarm.

Was it the police? His mouth dried in an instant. Surely if they'd found his hiding place for the candles they wouldn't call to question him on the phone. Would they?

Laura dropped the phone and rounded the counter at a near run. "You've got to get to the hospital. There's been a terrible accident."

THIRTEEN

Chase zipped the pickup into the front lot of Good Things In Wax.

"I'll grab it and be right back," he told Caitlin. "I don't want anyone in there to know what's going on." The minute they realized the candle in question was Forbidden Fantasy, Aunt Dot and Mom were sure to draw the conclusion that Korey was behind the drugs. He didn't want to alarm them—not yet. Not until he'd had a chance to get to Korey first.

He leaped out of the truck and dashed toward the door. What if someone had retrieved the candle from the sales counter since he'd put it there yesterday? He hadn't mentioned it to anyone. He'd intended to ask Willie to run it over to Ed Graham at the Candle Corner today. Only Willie hadn't shown up for work.

Chase ran through the front door to the cash register. He dropped to his haunches, searching through the cluttered shelf.

There. It was still where he'd tossed it yesterday. He stood, holding the candle in his hand.

Mom came through the door. "Chase, it's you. I'm glad you're here. Dot is having her hair done, and I've got to go to the—"

Chase cut her off as he dashed around the counter with the

candle at his side, out of easy view. "I can't stay. Sorry, Mom. Be back soon."

"But Chase!"

He ran out the door. She'd be angry with him until she found out what was going on. Then she'd understand.

"Got it," he told Caitlin as he leaped into the seat. "Let's get out of here. My mother tried to stop me."

Mom stood behind the door, watching him through the window. When she caught sight of Caitlin, her scowl transformed into a smile. She waved with enthusiasm.

Caitlin returned the wave as he put the truck in reverse and backed away. "Apparently she's not too upset with you."

"Only because she saw you."

He flashed Caitlin a quick grin, then sped down the road. When they were out of sight of the factory, he pulled the truck onto the grass beneath a line of blooming redbuds. This country road didn't get much traffic, so they'd have relative privacy. He jumped out of the truck.

Caitlin joined him behind the pickup. "How are we going to melt it?"

"We don't need to." Chase rummaged in the tool chest in the truck bed. "Here. We'll use these." He held up a hammer and a heavy putty knife.

He placed the candle on the edge of the blacktop road. As he hefted the hammer above the jar, Caitlin stopped him with a hand on his arm.

"Shouldn't you cover it up first?"

"Good point." Chase glanced around. He needed a rag, or a towel, or... His gaze fell on a wax-splattered canvas apron in the tool box.

"That will work," Caitlin said.

Chase wrapped the jar in the apron and set it on its side on the road. Then he smacked the bundle with the hammer. The sound of shattering glass broke the silence. Chase unfolded the apron.

He picked up the round lump of dark purple wax and knocked off a piece of glass. "Now let's see what's inside."

He placed the candle back on the blacktop and set the chisel against the wax. After two whacks, the lump broke cleanly into two.

Nestled in the center of the wax was a foil packet.

"What is it?" Caitlin's voice trembled as she searched Chase's face.

Stomach roiling, Chase rose. "It's heroin. Someone is planting heroin in our candles. And I'm afraid I know who."

Chase was quiet during the short ride to the middle school, lost in his own thoughts. And no wonder. He was probably trying to figure out how to tell his mother that Willie had been killed, and that their candles were being used to distribute drugs. Caitlin couldn't imagine what he must be feeling.

A good number of teachers' cars still filled the parking lot, and a trickle of students with bulging backpacks exited the school. Chase brought the truck to a stop beside a sidewalk leading to the front door.

"What are you going to do now?" she asked.

He glanced at the canvas bundle on the floor behind her seat. "I'm going to call Detective Jenkins and take this over to him. Then I'm going to go pay a visit to my cousin."

Pain shadowed his eyes, and Caitlin's heart wrenched. "I'll say a prayer for you."

His gaze softened. "Thanks. I appreciate that."

She nodded and opened the door.

He looked so sad, like he'd lost his best friend all over again. In a way, Caitlin supposed that was exactly what it felt like. All those feelings were being dredged to the surface as the nightmare of Kevin's death was replayed in the two recent murders. On impulse, she leaned across the armrest and brushed a kiss onto his cheek.

Mistake! A thrill zipped through her body as her lips touched his skin. Klaxon alarms sounded in her head. No innocent kiss between friends felt like that!

He felt it, too. A slow smile curved his lips. "What was that you were saying about a dateless year?" His voice held a husky note that sent heat into Caitlin's face.

She jerked upright and fumbled for the door handle. "Sorry. I was just—" Just what? *Shut up, Caitlin!* She practically leaped from the truck. No way to make a graceful exit now. She had to get out of here quickly, before she did anything else to embarrass herself.

Before she closed the door, he asked, "Listen, are you sure you don't need a ride after the practice?"

"Janie's supposed to be here." She managed to keep her voice even. "Unless she's being questioned by the police, I'm sure she will be. Hopefully, she won't mind taking me to the repair shop to get my car."

"Okay, but if she doesn't show up and you need a ride, you've got my number, right?"

He'd called her cell this morning to give her directions to the repair shop. She nodded. "I'll give you a call. I promise."

He paused. "Why don't you reconsider dinner?" He held up a hand. "Just a quick sandwich. You gotta eat before the concert, right?"

The way her stomach was quivering right now, she might never eat again. At least not for the next year.

She opened her mouth to refuse, but Chase's eyes stopped her. The imploring gaze he fixed on her held a mute appeal. He'd been through so much today, and the next few hours wouldn't get any easier for him. He probably needed a friendly

Romance? Suspense? Historical? The choice is yours!

Whether you prefer heartwarming romance, spine-tingling suspense or action-packed historical fiction, now you can find *Love Inspired*® novels to suit your taste and interests! And whichever series you choose, you can be sure that the books feature traditional conservative values, with themes of faith and the redemptive power of love.

Please allow us to send you two free books in the series you prefer. You're under no obligation to purchase anything. We hope you'll want to continue receiving them—always at a discount price and before they're available in bookstores—but that's entirely up to you.

Love Inspired® Romance
You'll enjoy these contemporary inspirational romances with Christian characters facing the challenges of today's world.

Love Inspired® Suspense
You'll be thrilled by these contemporary tales of intrigue and romance as the characters confront challenges to their faith ... and to their lives!

Love Inspired® Historical
With themes of romance, adventure and faith, these historical stories will sweep you away to another time and another world.

Along with your FREE BOOKS you'll also get **TWO FREE MYSTERY GIFTS!** We can't tell you what they are – that would spoil the surprise – but they're worth about $10!

Books received may not be as shown.

For novels in which family, faith and the redemptive power of love are central themes, return the reply card today!

WHICH FREE BOOKS SHOULD WE SEND YOU?

Affix one peel-off sticker (from the front of this insert) to indicate which series of *Love Inspired®* novels you'd prefer. We'll send you two free books in the series you select, and we'll also send you two free mystery gifts.

Accepting these books and gifts places you under no obligation to purchase anything, ever.

```
┌─────────────────────────────────┐
│                                 │
│   PLACE PEEL-OFF STICKER HERE   │
│                                 │
└─────────────────────────────────┘
```

FIRST NAME

LAST NAME

ADDRESS

APT #

CITY

STATE/PROV.

ZIP/POSTAL CODE

Offer limited to one per household. Offer not applicable towards series that subscriber is currently receiving. Please allow 4 to 6 weeks for delivery. Offer available while quantities last. **Your Privacy**– Steeple Hill Books is committed to protecting your privacy. Our Privacy Policy is available online at www.SteepleHill.com or upon request from the Steeple Hill Reader Service. From time to time we make our lists of customers available to reputable third parties who may have a product or service of interest to you. If you would prefer for us not to share your name and address, please check here ☐.

◄ DETACH AND MAIL – POSTAGE HAS BEEN PAID ►

® and ™ are trademarks owned and used by the trademark owner and/or its licensee.

LI-3P-09

Printed in the U.S.A.
© 2008 Steeple Hill Books

presence this evening. And truth be told, she'd prefer not to be alone, either. But she *would not* give up on the dateless year. She had to keep this attraction—which might be nothing more than rebound feelings—at bay. "Dutch treat?"

A grin replaced his worried expression for a second. "I'll pick you up at six-thirty."

She stepped away from the truck. "See you then."

Chase didn't pull away from the curb immediately, but watched Caitlin walk down the sidewalk. At the door, she turned and waved before disappearing inside.

He shifted into drive. His insides felt hollow, bereft of Caitlin's comforting presence. In the midst of all the turmoil this day had held, she'd been a pillar of quiet strength.

And what about that kiss? No doubt at all she felt the impact of that peck on the cheek. He'd seen the shock in her face.

Which proved this dateless year of hers was probably a good thing—for both of them. Because he could see himself falling hard for her, and it wouldn't work. She lived in Kentucky. Long-distance relationships never lasted long. So just staying friends was the best all the way around.

Except, deep inside, Chase knew his feelings for Caitlin had already gone beyond friendship. And the way he felt when she'd kissed his cheek proved it.

He shoved that thought away and focused on the task at hand. First, he had to get in touch with Detective Jenkins. He slipped the card Jenkins had given him out of his wallet. After he'd punched in the number on his cell, he turned on the speaker and set his phone in the center console so he could drive with both hands.

"Jenkins here." The detective's voice sounded diminished through the tiny speaker, with none of the force the man commanded in person. "That you, Hollister?"

Caller ID. "It is. Where are you?"

"In the parking lot behind Graham's store, waiting for that warrant. Why?"

"Because I've got something to show you. I'll be right there."

"That was perfect!" Seated in the front row on a metal folding chair, Caitlin clapped her hands. Her applause echoed off the walls of the empty gymnasium.

Up on a stage behind the basketball net, Nicky lowered her flute to her lap and beamed. "I didn't run out of breath, either."

"See, proper breath control really does make a difference, doesn't it?"

The girl's ear-to-ear grin brought a lump to Caitlin's throat. *Oh, Lord, hold off the news until after the concert tonight. She deserves some joy before her world crashes.*

Caitlin rose and went to stand at the edge of the stage while Nicky stored her flute in its case.

"I wonder where your mother is." Caitlin glanced at her watch. Four thirty-five. Janie had said she'd be here to watch the lesson. Was she being detained by the police?

Nicky didn't seem concerned. "She probably got tied up at work. Sometimes the next server doesn't show up on time and Mom gets stuck covering her shift." She handed Caitlin her flute case, dropped down to sit on the edge of the stage, and hopped to the floor.

"I hope she gets here soon. My car's in the shop, so I can't drive you home. In fact, I'm hoping she can give me a lift."

The wooden basketball court magnified the clack-clack of Caitlin's sandals as they made their way to the doors. Nicky scuffed her sneakers on purpose to make the loudest possible squeak on the polished floor. In spite of her gloomy thoughts, Caitlin grinned. Some things never changed.

Nicky pushed open the door and held it for Caitlin. "She's probably waiting for us out front now."

She wasn't. Only a few cars remained in the parking lot, and Janie's Camry wasn't among them. Nicky piled her backpack and instrument case on a bench near the front door and dropped onto it, unconcerned. Apparently, she'd been left waiting before. Caitlin glanced at her watch again. Uneasiness pricked at her. What would she do with Nicky if Janie were being detained by the police?

"Maybe we should call her," Nicky suggested.

"Okay."

"You'll have to use your phone." Disgust drew her features into a scowl. "I'm not allowed to have one until ninth grade."

Caitlin hid a grin as she retrieved her cell phone from her purse. "What's her number?"

She punched it in as Nicky recited it. But the call went straight to voicemail. She left a message explaining that they were finished with their lesson, and disconnected.

"Your mom must have her phone turned off," she told the girl.

"That's weird." The first hint of unease drew a line between Nicky's eyebrows. "She leaves it on all the time, even at work."

Caitlin remained silent. She doubted the police allowed you to have your cell phone on while you were being questioned.

The girl's mouth twisted sideways as she chewed on the inside of her lip. "Let me try my brother."

Caitlin handed over her cell phone and watched as Nicky pressed the numbers and then listened. The line in her forehead deepened. "He's not answering, either."

Her worry now fully apparent, she punched in another number. After a couple of seconds, she lowered the phone. "Dad's phone went straight to voicemail, too." Her voice wavered. "I'm not supposed to bother him at the store unless it's important."

Uh-oh. Caitlin couldn't let Nicky call the Candle Corner and hear that the police were there, searching the place. She held out her hand for the phone. "I can call. What's the number?"

Nicky swallowed before she gave it. Caitlin listened to the line ring, her shoulders tensing more with each second that passed. Someone finally answered on the fourth ring.

"Candle Corner, how may I help you?"

A woman's voice. Caitlin flashed a quick smile at Nicky. "Yes, I'm trying to reach Mr. Graham, please."

"He's not here right now. May I leave a message for him?"

"Do you know where I can reach him?" She matched the clerk's pleasant tone. "His daughter and I are waiting for his wife to pick us up, and she's overdue."

A pause. "I—I don't know if I should—" Caitlin's heart stuttered at the sudden worry in the woman's voice. "Actually, Ed and his wife are both at the hospital."

Shock whipped through Caitlin. Aware of Nicky's gaze glued to her face, she fought to keep her expression from changing. "I see."

"It's their son. Drew has been in a serious accident. Ed got a call from Janie and ran out of here, and I haven't heard from him since."

Oh, Lord, poor Nicky. Poor Janie. If Caitlin turned around to hide her face from Nicky, the girl would know something was wrong. She managed a quick smile. "How long ago was that?"

"About forty minutes." The woman hesitated. "I hope Ed will call with an update soon. If you want, I can give him your number."

The police hadn't arrived at the store yet, then. "That

will be fine." Caitlin recited her phone number, then disconnected the call.

Lord, what do I say to this girl? I can't tell her that her brother is in the hospital. That news shouldn't come from a stranger. And I certainly can't tell her that her father is going to be detained by the police any minute.

"Your dad had to leave to run an errand." That was true. "She's going to have him call me as soon as he gets back."

Nicky studied her face for a moment. "Okay. So we just sit here and wait?"

What a time to not have a car. Though she hated to bother Chase, given everything he had going on, she didn't have many options. She had to think of Nicky. And he did say to call if she needed anything.

"Let me call my friend," she told Nicky.

But Chase's phone went to voicemail, too.

He was probably busy pulling Willie's employment paperwork for the police. Or maybe he was talking to his employees, trying to pry some information out of them.

Maybe she should call a taxi. But before she did that, she'd try Chase one more time.

She pressed 411 and asked for Good Things In Wax. The operator connected the call directly, and a familiar female voice answered the phone.

A wave of relief forced Caitlin to the bench beside Nicky. "Hello, Mrs. Hollister. This is Caitlin Saylor. Is Chase available to come to the phone?"

"Caitlin!" The woman almost gushed. "How did you like the concert last night?"

So, apparently Chase's mother had not heard the news yet. "I enjoyed it very much, thank you." Did she sound too abrupt? She hoped not, but she didn't have the patience for pleasantries right now.

"And you're going to another concert tonight, I hear."

If Caitlin's situation weren't so serious, she might have laughed at the delight in Mrs. Hollister's voice. "Yes, ma'am." She paused. "Um, is Chase there? I'm in kind of a bind. My car is in the shop, and I'm stranded over at the middle school with a student. He mentioned if I needed a ride that I should call him, but he isn't answering his cell phone."

"I'm sorry. I haven't heard from him since he ran out of here. I thought he was still with you." Her tone became fretful. "I'd come get you myself, but my sister is having her hair done and my nephew isn't here, either. I can't leave the factory with no one in charge. And we're shorthanded, too. Even our deliveryman didn't show up today."

Caitlin gulped. She definitely hadn't been told the news. "That's all right. I can call a taxi."

"Oh, dear. I hate for you to do that."

Nicky's face grew more anxious with each passing minute. Caitlin nodded at the girl as she spoke. "We'll be fine, Mrs. Hollister. If you talk to Chase, please ask him to call me."

Caitlin disconnected the call. "I think we'd better call a taxi," she told Nicky.

The girl's face was pinched with worry. Caitlin's heart sank as she realized she wouldn't be grabbing a sandwich with Chase this evening, unless it was in the hospital cafeteria. And they wouldn't be alone. Without a doubt, she'd be tied up with Nicky this evening. And it definitely wouldn't involve any flute solos.

FOURTEEN

Chase pulled into the Candle Corner's rear lot and parked beside Detective Jenkins's car. Two deputies in cruisers pulled in behind him. He grabbed the canvas bundle and hopped out of the truck.

"I found a heroin packet in a candle," he announced without preamble.

Jenkins eyebrows rose. "What candle?"

"I'd pulled one out of the box yesterday afternoon before the shipment was delivered here." He jerked his head toward the store.

The detective's face went hard. "And you didn't tell me?"

Chase gulped. "I didn't remember until after I left Willie's house, so I went and got it. Take a look."

He set the bundle on the trunk of Jenkins's cruiser and carefully unfolded the wrapping. Shards of glass tinkled, and the two chunks of wax gaped apart. The foil packet lay embedded in one of them.

Jenkins glanced at one of the deputies. "Matthews, got some gloves?"

The man nodded and retrieved a set of thin rubber gloves from his car. Jenkins slid them on, picked up the wrinkled and creased foil packet, and peeled it open.

"Surprise, surprise." Jenkins voice was dry.

In the foil lay a dark colored lump. It was darker than Chase expected, and gunky-looking. Like a sticky chunk of coal.

"I thought heroin was white," he commented.

"Some is." Jenkins lifted the lump to his nose and sniffed. "This is called black tar heroin. Comes from Mexico." His lip curled with disgust. "Lucky us. We get the imported kind."

He dropped the packet back in the wax and refolded the bundle. "Kincaid, secure this. Matthews, you got the warrant?"

Matthews held a folded paper between his thumb and forefinger. "We had to interrupt the judge in court, but she signed it."

When Deputy Kincaid had stored the bundle, canvas apron and all, in a big plastic bag and locked it in the trunk, they rounded the building and went in the front. Chase followed along behind,

A half-dozen or so customers browsed in the small store. All of them looked up at the jangle of the bell over the door. A woman broke away from a pair in the rear corner and hurried forward, her business smile fading as she caught sight of the uniformed deputies.

"Can I help you, officers?"

Jenkins spoke in a pleasant tone. "We'd like to speak with Mr. Graham."

A quick glance around the small shop told Chase Graham wasn't here. His hands tightened into fists. Just wait until he got hold of that guy. He spied a doorway in the rear. Maybe Graham was in the back.

"I'm afraid he's not here." She clasped her hands in front of her waist. "His son was in an accident this afternoon. He's at the hospital."

"Let's get a verification of Graham's location, Kincaid." When the young deputy stepped aside to make a phone call, the detective nodded at Matthews.

Matthews extended the paper. "We have a warrant to search the premises, ma'am." He raised his voice and spoke to the others, who had all stopped shopping to stare openly at them. "I'm afraid I'm going to have to ask everyone who doesn't work here to leave."

Chase backed against a side wall as the customers filed past, their expressions curious. The door closed behind them with a jangle. The sales clerk, a woman Chase didn't know, examined the warrant. Her hand trembled when she handed it back to Matthews.

Jenkins spoke kindly. "What's your name?"

"L-Laura."

"And how long have you worked here, Laura?"

"About three years."

"Well, we need to ask you a few questions. What do you know about a candle called Forbidden Fantasy?"

Chase saw fear in her eyes. His gut tightened in response. She knew something.

"I don't know anything. Except..."

"Except what?" Jenkins prodded.

"We never sell the small-size Forbidden Fantasies." She waved toward a display of candles. "Never. Nobody buys them." Her gaze flickered to the rear doorway and back to his face. "But Ed sells big ones that he keeps locked in the office. Only to special customers."

The detective's eyebrows rose. "What kind of *special* customers?"

"People come in and ask for Forbidden Fantasy." She gulped. "Ed always goes into the back and gets a candle for them, sometimes more than one. And he doesn't ring them up on the register, either."

The slime ball. Chase set his teeth together.

Jenkins narrowed his eyes. "Surely you questioned that

strange behavior. Did he ever say anything by way of explanation?"

"He told me once that some people liked the really strong candles because they covered the smell of smoke or something." She shook her head. "I knew something strange was going on with those candles, but I never asked. I need this job."

"I understand. Where does he keep the candles he sells to these special customers?"

"I'll show you."

Now they were getting somewhere. They followed her into the back room, Chase at the rear of the line. They entered a crowded office dominated by a large steel cabinet along one wall. Detective Jenkins tried the handle. Locked. "Do you have a key?"

Laura shook her head. "Ed has the only one. I don't go in there."

Chase spoke up. "I've got a crowbar in the truck."

"So do we, sir," said Kincaid as he ran out.

The young deputy returned in minutes. The lock gave them a little trouble, but before long they had it opened.

Inside, a lot of empty space. Not a single candle.

Chase's stomach sank. Had Graham sold them all? Was a whole shipment of deadly candles circulating the streets of Little Nashville?

Deputy Matthews's phone chirped. He answered it, listened a moment, then told the detective, "Graham and his wife are at the hospital. And his kid was in an auto accident."

Jenkins nodded. "Okay, I'm heading over there. Matthews, get this place locked down and call in a search team. Get some dogs, too." Jenkins turned toward the door, but then noticed Chase. "You get back to the candle factory. We're heading there next, and I want to question every employee."

Chase's throat squeezed shut. "I understand."

Jenkins spoke to Kincaid. "Follow him and wait out front. Make sure nobody leaves. I'll call for a couple of deputies to back you up while I get over to the hospital and detain Graham." His glance slid to Chase. "No one is to leave the property, understood?"

Chase nodded. He wouldn't leave the property. But he intended to pay a visit to his cousin's trailer before the interrogators arrived.

When Jenkins started to leave, Matthews stopped him. "There's something else you should know, Detective. Graham's kid was in a car with another teenager when they crashed. The driver didn't make it. They were both high on heroin."

The world around Ed was made of thin, fragile glass. The slightest blow would shatter everything.

Robbie, Drew's best friend, a boy Ed had known for years, was dead. Drew himself lay beyond the double doors where he and Janie couldn't go. They were forced to sit on uncomfortable chairs in the surgery waiting room while doctors fought to save their son's life.

Janie's nails left half-moon gouges in his hand. "I don't understand." Her voice shook. "Why would he take drugs? Did we do something wrong, Ed?"

A parade of faces filed before his mind's eye. Anxious men who wouldn't look at him in the face as they shoved money in his hand and hurried away with their candles. Stringy-haired women, their skin stretched across skeletal bones, hungry only for more of the drug. His son wasn't like them, the riffraff, the dregs of humanity Ed sold his candles to.

Not yet.

He released Janie's hand and doubled over in the chair, writhing against the thoughts that battered his mind. It wasn't his fault! He didn't hurt Drew.

But that other guy, Lancaster. He'd heard about the profits to be made in southern Indiana, where a single supplier of black tar heroin was raking in money hand over fist. Ed had caught wind of Lancaster's dealings from a couple of his own customers. Word on the street said the guy was targeting teenagers, spreading around cheap samples to build his business, but Ed never imagined his own son would be one of his targets.

"I don't know, Janie." He clutched his head with his hands.

Suddenly Janie jerked upright, her eyes wide. "What time is it?"

Ed glanced at his watch. "It's about five."

"Oh, no." She fumbled in her purse and extracted her cell phone.

"You can't use that here." Ed pointed to the sign on the wall that indicated cell phones could interfere with the hospital's equipment.

She clutched the phone to her chest. "I have to go outside, then. I was supposed to pick up Nicky from her flute lesson at four." She whirled and headed for the elevators. "I'll be right back."

As she pushed the down button, the doors whooshed open. A man wearing a suit and tie stepped out. Janie tried to rush by him into the elevator, but he stopped her with an arm. "I'm looking for Ed Graham."

Not a doctor, at least not a surgeon. But maybe the man was some sort of hospital official with news of Drew. Ed stepped forward. "I'm Ed Graham."

The man's expression hardened. He opened a leather wallet and held a shiny badge toward him. "I'm Detective Mark Jenkins. I'd like to ask you some questions, Mr. Graham."

Ed's world shattered.

FIFTEEN

The bench where Caitlin and Nicky waited sat directly in the sun. There were no trees in the schoolyard, no shade at all. Caitlin mopped at her face with a damp tissue.

"I don't understand why her phone is off." Nicky mashed the end button on Caitlin's cell. She'd tried to call her mom at least ten times since they'd called for a taxi. "She never turns her phone off. Something's wrong."

"Maybe her battery died," Caitlin suggested.

Nicky gave her a sideways look. "Then why isn't she here, like she's supposed to be?"

Caitlin couldn't hold the girl's gaze. She'd never been good at deception. "She probably got tied up at work, like you said."

"But Dad's phone is off, too, and Drew isn't answering his." Nicky jumped up from the bench and paced down the walkway. "What if something's wrong? What if she had a wreck or something?" Tears filled the girl's eyes, and she wiped them away with the back of her hand. "What if she's dead?"

As the last word left her mouth, she started to sob.

Caitlin's heart wrenched. She wanted to assure Nicky that her mom was okay, but should she be the one to deliver bad news about her brother? On the other hand, wasn't it better that Nicky know the truth than worry that her mother was lying dead on the side of the road somewhere?

She went to stand before her. With a hand on each of the girl's shoulders, Caitlin dipped her head to force eye contact. "Nicky, listen to me. Your mother is not dead."

Nicky's breath shuddered as her chest heaved. "H-how do you know?"

"Because the lady at your father's store told me where she is. I didn't tell you because I didn't want to worry you."

The sobs tapered to a halt as she digested that news. "Where is s-she?"

"She's at the hospital, but she's not hurt." Caitlin squeezed her shoulders. "She and your father are there with your brother. He was in an accident." At least, Caitlin assumed Nicky's father was there. He might be in jail, but Caitlin wasn't going there with the girl.

Nicky's eyes went round. "Drew? Is he okay?"

"The lady at your father's store didn't know," she said. "She just told me both your parents were at the hospital with him. I'm sure your mom is distracted, and she's lost track of time. They probably had to turn their phones off."

Hurt flooded Nicky's eyes. "You lied to me."

Caitlin couldn't bear the look of betrayal. She dropped her head. "I know. I was trying not to worry you, and I upset you even more. I'm sorry. Please forgive me."

After a pause, Nicky leaned forward and hugged her gently. "It's okay. You meant well."

Tears stung Caitlin's own eyes as she returned the embrace. Then she pulled back. "Now that you know, I think we should call the hospital. They can probably put us through to your mom."

She held out her hand for the phone. As Nicky placed it in

her palm, a car pulled into the school's drive, heading toward them. Caitlin watched as a green Toyota pulled to a stop at the curb right beside them. The driver's door opened, and a familiar head appeared over the hood.

"Hey, I heard you needed a ride."

While the deputy waited in the front parking lot for backup, Chase went inside. He plowed straight through the shop, heading for the rear exit.

His mom stepped in front of him. "It's about time you showed up. Where have you been?"

She looked angry, and he couldn't blame her. "Mom, I'm sorry I've been gone today, but I've got to go talk to Korey."

"Oh, no you don't, mister." She planted her feet. "Something's going on, and you're going to tell me what it is."

Urgency tugged Chase toward the rear exit, but he couldn't leave without an explanation. He grabbed his mother's arm and pulled her into the office, then closed the door behind them.

"This is going to come as a shock."

He brought her up to speed quickly. Willie's death. Being questioned by the police. Finding heroin in the candle. The fact that several deputies were on their way to question everyone. "Before they get here I've got to talk to Korey. He's in his trailer."

"Why?" She looked shaken, and no wonder. "You don't think Korey has anything to do with this, do you?"

"Think about it, Mom. Whose idea was Forbidden Fantasy? Who set up the deal with the Candle Corner?" He glanced behind him, toward the door. Beyond it lay the pouring room. "Don't say a word to Aunt Dot. Not yet."

"She's my sister, Chase. Of course I'm going to tell her we've been distributing drugs in our candles." Her gaze grew stern. "I don't believe this of Korey. There's another explanation, and the police will find it."

If Chase had learned one thing over the past year, it was that you couldn't trust anyone. He didn't bother to filter the pain out of his voice. "I didn't believe it of Kevin, either."

Without another word, he left the office and headed toward the back of the factory as fast as he could go without breaking into a run. In the pouring room, he barely spared a nod at Aunt Dot and Irene, who hovered over several trays of votive containers on the central worktable.

When he exited the building, he did break into a run. Straight to Korey's trailer. As he ran, his anger built. How could his cousin betray his family like this? True, he'd never had any love for the candle-making business, but this was *family*. Not to mention all the lives he'd probably destroyed by distributing those drugs. And not just any drug. Heroin.

How many Forbidden Fantasy candles had they produced in the past year? A knot formed in his stomach as Chase pictured the neat figures he'd written on the P&L statement he'd just prepared. They'd produced a lot.

He leaped up the rickety stairs and pounded on the door with one hand while he tried the knob with the other. Unlocked. Chase pushed his way inside and slammed the door behind him. The trailer shook with the force.

Korey appeared from the bedroom, yawning. His hair stood up on one side and he still wore the same clothing he'd worn this morning. "Hey, Chase. What gives?"

Chase crossed the floor in three steps and grabbed the collar of the wrinkled T-shirt. He jerked his cousin forward until their faces were inches apart. "How could you do this?"

"Hey!" Korey placed his hands on Chase's chest and shoved. "What do you think you're doing?"

"You've been found out. There's a cop at the factory right now, and more on the way."

"A cop?" Korey raked his fingers through his disheveled

hair. "What are you talking about? Why are there cops at the factory?"

Chase stomped to the television set and grabbed the Forbidden Fantasy candle off the top. He shook it toward his cousin. "Because they found your heroin, Korey."

Korey's mouth gaped. "My heroin? I don't have any heroin."

"Oh, yeah? Well, do you want to explain how heroin got inside your candle?"

"You're not making any sense, dude." Korey held both hands out in front of him, palms facing Chase. "Calm down and tell me what you're talking about."

A whisper of doubt invaded Chase's righteous fury. Korey met his gaze and held it with clear eyes. Not the look of a deceiving drug dealer. This was his cousin, the guy he'd known all his life.

Chase shook his head to clear it. "I went by Willie's apartment this morning and found his body."

"What?" Korey staggered backward and landed against the doorframe with a thud. "Willie is dead?"

Chase studied his cousin's face. He couldn't be faking. His skin had gone pasty. *Thank the Lord. I didn't even want to think that Korey was a killer.*

He nodded. "Murdered. Throat cut, just like that guy in the park the other day. Just like Kevin. And the police found three Forbidden Fantasy candles in his trash."

Korey stumbled to the couch and collapsed onto it. "I don't understand. There were drugs in the candles?"

"Apparently. They'd been melted, not burned, and we figure he got the drugs out and probably used them. When Jenkins told me, I remembered I had an extra Forbidden Fantasy at the factory. I broke it open and found a packet of heroin inside."

Korey dropped his head into his hands. "This is unreal.

Drugs—inside my candles." He looked up. "But who put them there?"

Chase believed him at that moment. His cousin wasn't a good enough actor to pull off this kind of confusion.

He crossed to the couch and sat on the other end. "Since Forbidden Fantasy is your baby, I thought it must be you."

Korey straightened. He raised a hand, two fingers up. "Chase, it wasn't me. Boy Scout's honor. You know I never sit in on the pours anymore. I let the rest of you handle that." His gaze dropped, and he went on in the tone of one making a confession. "To be honest, the idea for an exclusive scent for the Candle Corner wasn't even mine."

Now it was Chase's mouth that gaped open. "It wasn't? Did Ed Graham approach you, then?"

"No. It was Alex's idea. He came up with it right after he was hired on at the factory. But Alex was too new to the candle-making business to know whether it was even doable. He asked me to go talk to Ed at the Candle Corner, and it all came together after that." He tossed an apologetic glance toward Chase. "I let everybody think it was my idea because…" He swallowed. "Our whole family is so into the business. You've come up with a bunch of new fragrances. Remember how proud Grandpa was when you created Dreamsicle? Mom and Aunt Bonnie, too. And then of course there's the whole college thing. You went, you graduated. But me?" He shook his head. "I've never been successful at anything."

Chase shook his head. He'd never realized Korey felt inferior to him in any way.

Korey continued. "I was shocked when Forbidden Fantasy sold so well." He took the jar from Chase's hands, twisted off the lid, and sniffed. His nose wrinkled. "The truth is, I think it stinks."

"I had no idea." Chase leaned against the back cushion. Apparently hc'd missed the boat all the way around. Misjudging his cousin in the matter of the drugs was just the beginning. He'd been completely blind to Korey's feelings of inferiority for years. "So you really were sick this morning." He dropped his gaze, unable to look his cousin in the eye. "When all this came down, I thought maybe you were crashing from a drug trip or something."

"No way!" A genuine laugh shook Korey's shoulders. "You want to know what I was doing last night?"

Chase nodded.

"I was online all night long talking to a girl."

"A girl?"

"She lives in Florida." Korey ducked his head with a shame-faced grin. "I met her on eHarmony. We've been chatting for a couple of months now, and it's starting to get serious. I really was just dog tired this morning."

Relief washed over Chase. That was the old Korey he knew, staying up all night to talk to a girl, then ducking out of work the next day to catch up on his sleep. He stood, grabbed his cousin by the arm and pulled him into a hug. "I'm sorry, man. I shouldn't have doubted you."

Korey thumped him hard on the back before releasing him. "Since I can't see Irene or either of our moms as drug dealers, does that mean Ed Graham and Alex are in together on a drug-selling scheme?"

"I have a feeling that's exactly what it means. And Willie must have been in on it, too. I think that means either Alex or Graham murdered him."

"Alex introduced me to Willie when we decided to hire a delivery guy. Said he'd known him for a while and would vouch for him." Korey shook his head. "He really manipulated me all the way around, didn't he?"

"He manipulated all of us." Chase set his teeth together.

He'd employed a drug dealer at the least, a murderer at the worst. "Detective Jenkins is on his way to talk to Graham now. I think we should let him handle Alex, too. I'll go tell the deputy what we suspect."

Chase left Korey in the trailer to get cleaned up, and then made his way back to the factory. As he approached the back door, he noticed that Alex's car was gone. Now that he thought of it, he didn't remember seeing the car when he stormed out of the building toward Korey's trailer.

He went inside to find his mom talking with Irene and Aunt Dot. All three women looked up, their expressions stricken.

Aunt Dot started to speak. "Chase, I—"

He cut her off with a raised hand. "I just talked to Korey, and everything's cool." He hardened his voice. "But where's Alex?"

Understanding dawned on all three faces.

"He ran out of here about twenty minutes ago," Irene said. "Had to run an errand or something."

"Odd. He didn't say anything to me." Mom tilted her head and looked at Irene. "He came into the office while I was on the phone." She snapped her fingers. "Oh, Chase, I forgot to tell you. Caitlin Saylor called. She was stranded at the middle school with a student and needed a ride. Dot wasn't back yet, so I couldn't leave. She said she would get a taxi, and asked me to have you call her."

Caitlin. Every muscle in Chase's body tensed into statue-like stillness. When he gave her the Forbidden Fantasy candle, Willie saw him do it. And Alex saw her carrying it.

Neither of them knew she didn't leave with it.

"Mom?" His voice caught in his throat. "Was Alex standing in the office when Caitlin called?"

"Why, yes. I believe he was. He must have left right after that."

Chase sprinted to the front. He needed to talk to Deputy Kincaid *now*.

SIXTEEN

Caitlin eyed the man she'd met yesterday at Chase's factory. He'd been chopping wax and bulging his muscles on purpose, for her benefit. That kind of guy made her nervous— handsome in a rugged way, fully aware of the fact, and unscrupulous in using his looks to his advantage.

"Alex, right?"

His smile brightened as he came around the front of the car toward them. "That's right. Mrs. H sent me over to give you a lift. Said something about being stranded with a student?" His gaze slipped over to Nicky and his eyes narrowed. "Hey, don't I know you?"

Nicky studied him a minute, then her face cleared. "Yeah, I've seen you talking to my dad. Ed Graham at the Candle Corner? I'm his daughter, Nicky."

"Are you serious?" He threw back his head, laughter erupting from his throat. "This is great. Yeah, kid. Your dad and me go way back."

He pulled Nicky into a sideways hug, then left his arm draped across her shoulders. Caitlin's stomach tensed. She didn't like the way he touched Nicky. There was something too familiar, too eager in his actions. And the fact that he knew Ed Graham made her distrust him even more.

He gestured toward his car. "Ladies, Alex's limo is at your service. Where do you need to go?"

"I really appreciate the offer," Caitlin told him, "but we've called a taxi. It should be here any minute."

"Aw, don't worry about that. Taxi drivers steal each other's fares all the time. They're used to showing up and finding nobody there. C'mon. Hop in."

The gaze he fixed on her held an intensity that felt…wrong. She searched the main road and jiggled the cell phone in her hand. Where was that taxi? "It seems rude to take off when they're probably on the way."

"I'm telling you, it's okay. Besides, I'm a bargain, as far as taxis go." He grinned. "I'm free."

Nicky turned a worried look on her. "I really want to get to the hospital and check on my brother. How much longer will it be before the taxi gets here?"

"Your brother's in the hospital?" Was his expression too concerned to be genuine?

Nicky sniffed. "My mom and dad are there now, and that's where we're going."

"Well, that settles it." Alex's hand tightened around Nicky's shoulder. The gesture sent alarm shooting through Caitlin. "Taxis in this town are notoriously slow. You could easily be waiting here for another hour."

Caitlin had no intention of getting into that car with Nicky. Her grip on the phone tightened as she spoke in her firmest tone. "We appreciate the offer, Alex, but we're going to wait for the taxi." She stared hard into Nicky's eyes, willing the girl to go along with her. "I'm sure it will be here any minute."

Alex's chest expanded. His gaze scanned the building behind Caitlin as he blew out a long, slow breath. With his free hand, he reached behind his back and under his shirt. "You're determined to make this hard on me, aren't you?"

Caitlin knew what he was reaching for before it appeared—a gun. He pressed the barrel into Nicky's side, pulling her firmly against him.

Fear snatched the breath from Caitlin's lungs. Nicky's mouth hung open, her eyes wide with sudden panic.

"Come on, ladies. We're going for a ride." He rounded the front of the car, pulling Nicky with him toward the driver's door.

Caitlin stood rooted to the sidewalk, her stunned brain trying to figure out what action to take.

"Open the door," Alex instructed Nicky.

When the girl had done as he commanded, Alex eyed Caitlin over the roof. "Are you coming, or are you going to let me take her alone?"

Horror slid down Caitlin's spine. She had no choice. She took a step toward the car, but he stopped her.

"Drop your phone in the grass. And get your purse. You'll need it."

Why? But she couldn't force the word from her throat, not while he pressed a gun in Nicky's side. Caitlin let her cell phone fall from her fingers, her hopes plunging to the ground along with it. She whirled and ran back to the bench where they'd left their belongings. As she did, she scanned the rows of windows in the school. Was anybody watching? Could anybody see what was going on?

Lord, let someone see us and call the police!

Her purse lay on the bench beside Nicky's backpack and instrument case. Gathering them all up, she turned in time to see Nicky crawling over the center armrest in the Toyota's front seat. Alex's arm pointed inside the car, his gun trained on the girl.

Dread swelled like floodwaters inside Caitlin as she returned to the car.

Alex nodded toward the back door. "Get in."

She did as she was told and slid into the backseat. At the same moment she sat, Alex ducked into the front.

"Slide over to the middle." He adjusted the rearview mirror, ice-blue eyes visible in the oblong reflection. "That way I can keep an eye on you. And don't do anything stupid. A gun isn't my preferred weapon, but I'll use this one on the girl if you make me."

From the front seat, Nicky's breath came hard and noisy, big gulps of air like someone desperate not to cry.

What do I do?

Caitlin's brain refused to work. What did Alex want with them? He'd showed up at the school to pick her up, supposedly sent by Chase's mother. Did he know Nicky was there, too? She could think of several reasons for a man to abduct a woman and a child, all of them horrible. She needed a plan, a way to escape. Or at least a way to defend herself and Nicky. Why hadn't she gotten some mace, as Jazzy suggested before she left home?

She did have a knife in her purse. Daddy had always carried a pocket knife, and when she moved out on her own Caitlin discovered a dozen uses for the handy little tool. The small three-and-a-half-inch blade wouldn't be much defense against a gun, but it was the best she could do at the moment.

Her purse rested on the seat beside her, behind Nicky. Keeping her gaze fixed on his profile, she slipped her hand slowly inside the bag. Her fingers encountered her wallet, a comb, a miniature can of hairspray, a tube of lip gloss. Why did she have to carry so much junk?

The Toyota's engine roared to life.

"I think we'd better have the windows up, don't you?" The conciliatory tone in Alex's voice made Caitlin want to throw up.

As the window beside Caitlin glided upward, a familiar sound reached her ears. Her cell phone was ringing in the grass.

Her fingers touched the hard plastic of the knife's handle.

"Come on, Caitlin. Answer the phone."

Chase paced the parking lot, his cell to his ear. Kincaid was trying to get in touch with Jenkins. At the fifth ring, Caitlin's voice sounded in his ear. Chase's heart leapt.

"Hello, this is Caitlin. Sorry I've missed your call, but if you'll leave—"

He slammed the cover down. "Voicemail," he told the deputy.

Kincaid spoke into his phone. "Detective, the girl isn't answering." Pause. "Yes, sir, she called Hollister's mother about half an hour ago looking for a ride."

Chase's fingers itched. He clenched and unclenched his fists, then couldn't restrain himself any further. He snatched the cell away from the deputy's ear. He needed to talk to the detective himself.

"Jenkins, the person responsible for putting the drugs in the candles is Alex Young, one of my employees. Who knows what else he's done, but a woman and a girl may be in danger. We've got to find them *now.*"

"Hollister, stop shouting in my ear." Jenkins's stern voice matched Chase's for volume. "Now, calm down and tell me what you're talking about."

Chase closed his eyes. *Getting excited won't help.* With iron control, he kept his tone even as he relayed to the detective everything he and Korey had deduced. He went on to describe his mother's conversation with Caitlin.

"Yesterday, when she was here, I gave her one of the candles that was supposed to be delivered to the Candle Corner." He closed his eyes. He'd put her in danger. If anything happened to Caitlin, it would be his fault.

He set his jaw and continued. "Willie and Alex both saw her with the candle. Now Willie's dead, and Alex is gone. And he knew Caitlin was at the middle school."

"You *think* he knew. But he might be down at the DMV renewing his driver's license for all you know."

Chase ground gravel beneath his foot. Everything inside him cried out that Caitlin's life was in jeopardy. Why did Jenkins sound so rational, so calm, when he ought to be putting out an APB to find them?

He ran a hand across his mouth. "Did I tell you who the girl with Caitlin is? It's Ed Graham's daughter. Didn't you tell me you don't believe in coincidences?"

The line was silent for a moment. "All right. I'll get someone on it. I'm going to need any information you have on this Young character, including a description."

"I'll get his personnel file. We made copies of his ID, so I have his driver's license picture."

Chase tossed the phone to Kincaid as he ran for the front door of the factory. Inside, his mom and the others rushed toward him as he sped into the office.

"Chase, what's going on?"

Chase jerked open the file drawer in his desk. "The police need copies of Alex's ID."

Korey arrived then, and Aunt Dot ran to his side, threw her arms around him and buried her face in his shoulder, sobbing. Irene stood nearby, clasping and unclasping her hands.

"What's going on?" He looked to Chase for an explanation as he patted his mother's back.

"Alex is missing, and so is Caitlin, the girl I went out with last night." Chase grabbed the folder with Alex's name on the tab and slammed the drawer closed. "You stay with them, okay? The police want statements from everyone."

Korey nodded. "Go. I'll cover things here."

Chase stopped long enough to plant a kiss on his mom's cheek. "Say a prayer for her."

"I will."

He ran through the gift shop. As he exited the factory, two cruisers pulled into the parking lot. The backup Jenkins had dispatched. Chase headed toward his pickup, but Kincaid stepped into his path.

He held up the folder. "I've got to get this to Detective Jenkins."

"I can take it to him."

He held out a hand, but Chase clutched the folder to his chest. "You have to stay here and question everyone. Jenkins needs this now."

The man's face grew stern. "The detective told me to keep everyone here."

Frustration bubbled inside Chase. *Stay calm. He's just trying to do his job.* But he couldn't stay here. He would explode if he didn't do something to find Caitlin and that girl.

The force of his feelings surprised him. Had it really been only yesterday that she'd walked through the door to his factory and charmed him with that Kentucky accent? They'd shared more in the short time they'd known each other than he and Leslie did in the months they'd dated. Caitlin's dimpled grin loomed in his mind, and his heart twisted in response. He'd never met anyone like her.

He couldn't stand by and do nothing while she was in danger.

"Am I under arrest, deputy?"

His gaze wavered. "Well, no."

"Then I'm leaving." Chase strode toward his truck and spoke over his shoulder. "You can call Jenkins and tell him I'm on my way to the hospital with the file he requested."

But I'm going to make one stop first.

SEVENTEEN

"Where are you taking us?"

Caitlin's voice betrayed none of the terror she felt. In the front passenger seat, Nicky was stock still. Amazing that she managed to hold her emotions in check with a gun pointing in her direction. Caitlin laid a comforting hand on her shoulder and felt the girl press backward into it.

"We're going to your hotel." Alex steered with his right hand. The left lay across his lap, with the gun trained on Nicky.

So Alex was the one responsible for planting drugs in the candles at Chase's factory, not his cousin Korey. If only she could get in touch with Chase.

What is he going to do to us at the hotel?

With her right hand, Caitlin touched the knife where she'd slipped it onto the seat beneath her purse. It was intended to open packages and slice apples. What good would such a small blade be against a man like Alex? And even if it did startle him long enough to give them a chance to run, she didn't dare use it while the gun was pointed in Nicky's direction.

Could she use it at all?

Thou shalt not kill.

The car pulled into the parking lot of the Nashville Inn. "How do you know where I'm staying?"

The rearview mirror reflected a cold smile. "A friend told me."

Did he mean Chase? No, Chase wouldn't have told Alex where she was staying. At least, not on purpose. But he obviously knew. He drove straight to the side entrance, the one closest to Caitlin's room. Glass still littered the asphalt where her car had been parked last night.

"You broke into my car, didn't you?"

He shook his head as he pulled around to the rear side of the building, out of sight of the road. "Not me."

When the car stopped, Alex cut the engine and pocketed the keys. Caitlin surveyed their surroundings. Her heart sank. Not a soul in sight, and the curtains were closed on every window on the back side of the hotel.

Alex opened his door. The gun's direction did not waver as he slipped his free hand beneath Nicky's arm and jerked her toward him. "Bring your room key but leave everything else," he told Caitlin as he jerked the girl over the center armrest and outside.

Nicky let out a choked sob that sent an ache through Caitlin's heart. She did as directed.

He marched Nicky to the side door and stood behind it. "Open it, and make sure nobody's in the hallway."

No one was. Caitlin led the way down the corridor to her room, moving slowly as directed, with Alex and Nicky close behind her. If only a housekeeper was making her rounds right now. Or a hotel guest was looking out the door. But the hallway was deserted and remained that way while Caitlin unlocked her door and led their captor inside.

Alex released Nicky with a forward shove. The girl stumbled, but then ran to throw her arms around Caitlin. Her sobs grew loud.

"Shut up," Alex told her, and waved the gun in their direction.

His gaze circled the room and came to rest on her shopping bags piled on the dresser. One long stride took him there, where he snatched up one of the bags. The one from Good Things In Wax. He turned to the bed and dumped the contents on the mattress.

Alex's expression became hard, his eyes glittering like a crazed animal. "Unwrap them."

Fresh fear seized Caitlin by the throat. He thought she still had the Forbidden Fantasy candle. What would he do when he discovered she didn't? She slowly released Nicky and went to the bed. With trembling hands, she unwrapped a candle. Green Apple.

"Not that one," he snapped. "The other one."

Her throat completely dry, she tried to swallow as she peeled the wrapping off the second jar.

When Alex caught sight of the creamy, white vanilla candle, a foul string of words dirtied the air. He crossed the space between them in a single step and shoved the gun beneath her chin, forcing her head back until she looked him in the eye. Blood pounded in Caitlin's ears as her sight went dim with terror.

His growled whisper was as foul as his cursing. "Where is the purple candle Chase gave you?"

"I—I don't have it." Cold gun metal brutalized the soft skin at the top of her neck. "I didn't like the smell, so Chase took it back."

For one second, silence pressed against her ears while his eyes burned into hers. Then Alex started to laugh.

"Willie broke into your car to get that candle. When it wasn't there, I tried to send him after you, but he wouldn't go." He backed up, shaking his head. "He's dead, you know. I killed him because he refused. Turns out the effort would have been futile anyway. I killed a man because of something you never had."

He killed Willie?

The temperature in Caitlin's core dropped to freezing. Alex was not just a kidnapper. He was a killer.

And he's going to kill us.

Nicky, eyes wide with terror, began to shriek. The sound sliced through the hush in the room and echoed off the walls. Alex sprinted the few feet between them.

"Shut up!" His hand drew back, and before Caitlin could reach them, he slapped her across the face. The force of his blow knocked her sideways against the bed. The shrieking stopped.

Caitlin dropped to the bed, using her body as a shield. She stared with horror at Alex. "You're a monster."

His eyes narrowed. "You'd do well to keep that in mind."

Jenkins slipped his cell phone back in the case on his belt. He was getting nowhere questioning Graham here in the hospital, especially not with the man's wife clutching his arm, her face full of anguish. And he was about to level another blow on her.

I hate this part of the job.

He crossed the room and stood in front of Graham's chair, forcing the man to look up at him. "Are you acquainted with a woman named Caitlin Saylor?"

Graham's wife released his arm and leaped to her feet. "Yes. We met her yesterday. She's a flute teacher from Kentucky, and she was nice enough to give our daughter a couple of lessons." Mrs. Graham clutched her cell phone in her hand. "I was just going to call her when you arrived. Nicky is with her now, and I was supposed to pick them up at four, but when Drew—" She stopped. Her stricken gaze traveled to the closed doors to the surgery hall.

Jenkins couldn't look at her. Instead, he stared at Graham. "And how well do you know Alex Young?"

The man's expression grew guarded. "Not well. We've had a few business dealings."

Jenkins kept his voice dry. "So I understand." He turned to Mrs. Graham and spoke softly. "Ma'am, I hate to bring you even more bad news, but I've just discovered that Miss Saylor and your daughter may be missing." He looked back at Graham, waiting for the man's reaction to his next revelation. "And so is Alex Young."

Graham's response was everything Jenkins could have hoped for. He reared backward in the chair, a look of horror stealing over his features. In the next instant he was on his feet, both hands on Jenkins's arm in a bruising grip.

"You've got to find them! Alex Young is a murderer. You've got to find him before he hurts my daughter."

Mrs. Graham gasped, and wilted. Jenkins caught her just before she hit the floor.

Chase's pickup screeched to a halt in front of the middle school. Not a soul in sight. One car in the parking lot, but no driver. And nobody waiting for a ride.

He shoved the gearshift into Park and jumped out without turning the engine off. The doors to the school were locked.

"Is anybody in there?" His fists beat on the glass while he stared down the deserted hallway. "Come on, somebody's got to be in there."

A head poked out of the office doorway on the left. Older, but familiar. The vice principal.

"Mr. Traxel!" Chase threw his weight against the locked handle. "Open up. I need to talk to you."

The man came to the door and after a moment of studying Chase through the window, opened it from the inside. Chase grabbed the door and jerked it toward him.

"I remember you." Mr. Traxel pointed a finger in his face. "Hollister, right?"

"Yes, sir. I'm looking for someone, a woman. She was here earlier with one of your students, Nicky Graham."

His face brightened. "Ah, Nicky. Bright girl. Plays in the band. We're having a concert here tonight, you know."

Chase forced himself to reply politely. "Yes, sir, I know. My friend, a blond lady, was helping Nicky with her flute here this afternoon. Did you happen to see them?"

"I did, in fact. They were in the gymnasium practicing. But they left quite a while ago."

"How long?"

Mr. Traxel glanced at his watch. "At least an hour."

Chase dropped his chin to his chest. Caitlin had called his mom forty-five minutes ago. Mr. Traxel's information was of no help at all.

He spun around. "Thanks anyway, sir."

On his way back to the truck, he spied something in the grass. Something pink. He stooped to examine it. A cell phone. *Could it be…*

He snatched his own and dialed Caitlin's number.

The pink one rang.

He scooped it up and dashed to the pickup. Once inside, he scanned the previous calls on his cell phone for Jenkins's number, then pressed redial as he pulled away from the curb.

The detective answered immediately. "Hollister, what part of 'do not leave the property' don't you understand? My deputy said you ran out of there saying something about bringing me Young's file."

"I have it." Chase glanced at the folder on the seat beside

him. "But I decided to swing by the middle school on the way, just to see if maybe they were still here."

The middle school was in the opposite direction from the hospital, but the detective didn't question his explanation. "And?"

"The vice principal saw Caitlin and Nicky here about an hour ago, but he didn't see them leave. I found Caitlin's cell phone. It was in the grass near the front of the school."

"Tell me you didn't pick it up."

Chase slapped a hand on the steering wheel. He'd been so caught up in tracking Caitlin down, he'd forgotten not to touch the evidence. "Yeah, I did."

A loud sigh sounded in his ear. "This is why I can't stand civilians getting involved in my investigations."

Chase could have kicked himself. "Sorry, Detective."

"Where are you now?"

"Turning onto Washington Street, on my way to the hospital."

"Turn around. I'm heading for the station. I'll be there in five minutes and I want that file on my desk waiting for me."

Chase flipped on his turn signal in preparation for a U-turn. "Yes, sir."

If only someone would step into the hall in time to see Alex shove a sniffling Nicky toward the exit. Caitlin stayed close to her, afraid to let go of Nicky's hand for fear she'd begin screaming again. No telling how Alex would react. Droplets of blood splattered the front of the girl's shirt from his vicious slap, and both lips were split and swollen at one edge.

At the end of the hallway, Alex cracked the exit door and stuck his head out. "Come on."

Nicky sobbed as he yanked her through. Caitlin stumbled over the doorjamb in her attempt to keep up. At the car, Alex shoved Nicky inside, the gun still trained on her. With a glance at Caitlin, he jerked his head toward the rear. "Get in. Same place as before."

He wasn't even pretending to be nice anymore. The revelation that she didn't have the Forbidden Fantasy candle, that she'd never had it, had peeled away the thin veneer of charm he'd assumed earlier. A lump of cold fear grew in her middle. An image of the deliveryman she'd met yesterday, Willie, rose in her mind. Alex had killed him. She had to assume he wouldn't hesitate to kill again.

She climbed into the backseat and slid to the center.

As Alex navigated through the parking lot, a family exited the hotel's front entrance. Husband, wife, two young boys. Caitlin eyed the door beside her.

She could punch the automatic lock, open the handle, and roll out of the car, screaming for help. They weren't going very fast. It might spook Alex long enough for her to get away.

But what about Nicky?

Could Caitlin convey her plan in time? If she shouted at Nicky to *run now*, would the girl be able to react quickly enough to escape along with her? What if Caitlin got out, but Alex sped off with Nicky still in his car?

At that moment, Nicky's hand crept backward toward her. Caitlin grabbed it and returned the girl's desperate grip. All thoughts of escaping on her own evaporated. She couldn't risk leaving Nicky. Who knew what Alex would do to the child before the police caught up with him? *If* they caught up with him.

The car pulled from the parking lot onto the main road and gained speed. They were heading away from town. Caitlin took a last look out the back window at the family leaving the hotel.

A sob caught in her throat. Would she ever have the family

she'd always longed for? She closed her eyes, and Chase's face was so clear she almost felt she could reach out and touch him. Or better yet, step into his warm embrace. She would be safe there. Even though she'd only known him for a day and a half, Caitlin knew Chase would keep her safe if he could.

But Chase couldn't help her. She was at the mercy of the monster in the front seat.

"Where are we going now?"

His eyes flashed in the rearview mirror. "Just shut up. I have to think."

Nicky squeezed her hand. The girl was trembling. Caitlin didn't feel too steady herself. She had no comfort to offer Nicky, no strength on which the girl could rely.

"My grace is sufficient for thee, for my strength is made perfect in weakness." One of her memory verses from vacation bible school years ago floated through her mind.

Alex's voice sliced into her thoughts. "It was about time to blow this town anyway, I guess. Things are getting too hot around here. A shame, though." His head turned as he looked toward Nicky. "Your daddy and me, we've made some good money in the past year."

Nicky's head jerked sideways, eyes round as melons. A fresh drop of blood had seeped from the cut on her lip. It glistened on her chin.

"Don't listen to him, Nicky." Caitlin glared into the mirror.

He caught her glance and laughed. "Yeah, that's right, kid. Your old man is a business associate of mine. You didn't know that, did you? We've had a good thing going with those Forbidden Fantasy candles. But I guess it was inevitable that someone would find us out sooner or later."

"Stop it, Alex." Caitlin made her voice as stern as she dared.

"What do you mean?" Nicky's voice wavered.

"Heroin. Your daddy's a dirty old drug dealer, little girl."

Caitlin squeezed Nicky's hand. The poor, poor girl.

Angry splotches of red stained Nicky's face. "I don't believe you."

His shoulders heaved with a laugh. "Believe what you want, kid. I don't care one way or another. Oh, it wasn't his idea. I'll take credit for that brainstorm. But he jumped at the chance when I laid it out for him."

Nicky's expression went stony. She released Caitlin's hand and faced forward.

Caitlin connected again with Alex in the rearview, and she poured as much poison into her gaze as she could. Wasn't it enough that he'd kidnapped and physically abused the girl? Did he have to be mentally cruel as well?

Alex's cold laugh filled the car. The hair on Caitlin's arms rose. The man was evil. He had absolutely no sense of compassion at all.

And this heartless man held their lives in his hands.

EIGHTEEN

Jenkins entered the small conference room where Ed Graham had been taken. Graham, slumped over the round table, jerked upright at Jenkins's entrance.

"Any word on my daughter?"

The man's reddened eyes had puffed up like a pair of blowfish. He looked ten years older than he had when they left the hospital twenty minutes ago. Jenkins almost felt sorry for him. Almost.

He slapped a notepad on the table before he sat. "Not yet. We've activated the AMBER Alert system, and the state police are watching every road for Young's car. I've got deputies combing this town. We'll find her."

Graham gulped and nodded. "And my son. Will you tell me when he's out of surgery?" His eyes begged.

Jenkins pulled out a chair and lowered himself into it. "You've still got your cell phone, haven't you?"

Graham nodded.

"I'll let you take a call from your wife."

His head drooped forward. "She probably won't call me."

Judging by the fury Jenkins had seen in her eyes when they left her at the hospital in the care of a female deputy, Graham might be right.

"My deputy will call me." He reached over and flipped on the digital recorder. "Just so you know, I'm recording this conversation. I'm going to use whatever you tell me. Not only to help find your daughter, but to put you behind bars. Do you understand?"

Graham didn't look up, but he nodded.

"Out loud, please."

"Yes, I understand."

"Thank you. Now, tell me about the candles."

Graham lifted his head. "My wife and kids don't know anything. You've got to believe that."

Jenkins spoke softly. "Apparently, your son knows something."

The man's head shook so violently his hair tossed back and forth. "He didn't get that stuff from me. There was a new guy in town, trying to sell to kids."

"Lancaster."

"Yeah, him. I found out about him from a couple of…" Graham gulped. "My clients. I told Alex he needed to go have a talk with the guy. Instead, Alex killed him."

Jenkins clicked his pen. He started an ink swirl on the pad, then asked, "How'd you get hooked up with Alex Young?"

"He approached me a little over a year ago." Graham sat back in the chair. "Came into the store, said he'd just moved to town from Phoenix. We met for drinks a couple of times. Then one night he told me his idea about the candles. He said he had some contacts out west who could get black tar heroin direct from Mexico."

Jenkins set his teeth together. "Go on."

"He said planting heroin in candles would be easy. Just melt the wax, shove in a sealed foil pouch, and wait for the candle to harden. But the more we talked about it, we realized we couldn't use just any candle. They'd have to be special candles, removed from inventory and held in the back until someone asked specifically for them. That way, an innocent person wouldn't get hold of one by mistake. Also, it would have to be a dark candle you couldn't see through.

"At first it was just beer talk, you know? Just a crazy scheme he'd dreamed up, something to pass the time over a pitcher or two." He laid his hands flat on the table, fingers splayed, and stared at them. "Or, that's what I thought. Then that dead guy turned up in the park last year."

Jenkins straightened. "Kevin Duncan?"

Graham nodded. "About a month later, Alex came into the store and told me things were falling into place. He'd been given the dead man's job at Good Things In Wax, and started the ball rolling. I was going to get a call from someone there with a deal to manufacture an exclusive scent just for my store."

"Did he admit to killing Duncan?"

"Not in so many words." Graham met his gaze and held it. "But I know he did. He mentioned teaching the guy a lesson about being uncooperative. I think he must have approached him with the scheme, and Duncan refused. So he killed him to keep him quiet, and to take his place at the factory. He shot him up with heroin first to make it look like he was a user."

Jenkins's pen circled over an inky bull's eye he'd doodled on the paper. *What do you know? Hollister may have been right about his buddy all along.*

"You've got to find him, Detective." Desperation made his voice husky. "Before he hurts my little girl."

"I understand you received a shipment of loaded candles from Good Things In Wax yesterday. Where are they?"

Graham hesitated only a moment. "They're over at my place. We've got a half acre of uncleared land in the backyard, and there's an old lean-to back there. I stashed the candles there this morning, after Alex called and told me he wasn't able to recover one that went missing yesterday at the factory. Hollister gave it to that flute teacher."

Jenkins nodded. "So, are you saying Young broke into Miss Saylor's car last night to try to get the candle back?"

"No, Willie Evans did that." Graham dug at his eyes with his thumb and forefinger. "He's the other person who's in on the deal. He used to be one of my, uh, customers. When Alex heard Hollister's company was looking to hire a driver, he figured it would be good to have another man on the inside there. He asked me if I knew of someone we could trust, and that's how Willie got the job at the factory. He's an addict, but he keeps it under control enough to do his job. And he'll do just about anything in return for a couple of free fixes."

Interesting. He used the present tense when referring to Evans. "I paid a visit to Evans's apartment earlier today. He's dead."

Graham started, eyes wide. "Overdose?"

Not a faked reaction. The man hadn't heard. "Nope. His throat was slit, just like the two in the park."

Graham dropped his head into his hands. "I didn't mean for any of this to happen." His voice was muffled by his fingers.

"Maybe you should have considered that before you struck a deal with a murdering drug dealer." Jenkins rose. "I'll be back." The man needed some time to think about the reward his actions had reaped.

NINETEEN

The stained carpet in front of Detective Jenkins's desk bore evidence that Chase's feet were not the first to pace there. He wandered back and forth along a five-foot trail like a caged lion, ready to pounce at the first glimpse of his prey.

The prey finally stepped into the room. Chase snatched the folder off the desk's littered surface and whirled to thrust it into Jenkins's chest.

"I thought you said you needed this immediately. I've been waiting here twenty minutes."

Jenkins's eyebrows rose. "You're not supposed to be here at all, but you refuse to do as you're told."

The man's cold expression irked him, but Chase bit back a sharp retort and forced himself to wait silently as the detective rounded his desk, sat, and reached for the telephone.

"Matthews, where are you?" A long pause. "That's not good." A shorter pause. "Have somebody get a sample, and send it to the lab. Then get over to Graham's place. He says there's a cargo of candles in a lean-to at the back of the property. Call me the minute you have them."

Chase ground his teeth. *Forget those stupid candles. What are you doing to find Caitlin?* He wanted to demand an answer, but he'd learned last year that demands got him nowhere with Jenkins. Instead, he focused on not exploding while the detective called someone else.

"Any update on the Graham boy?" He listened. "I see. How's the mother doing?" A nod. "Good, good. Keep me posted."

He's doing this on purpose just to irritate me. Well, Chase's patience would only last so long. Then he'd blow like Mount St. Helens.

Fortunately, Jenkins hung up the phone and pulled the folder toward him. "Let's see what we have here." He opened the file and thumbed through the short stack of papers inside.

"There's his identification." Chase leaned over and lifted a sheet from the folder. "See, it's his Santa Fe driver's license, which is all he had when he first came to town. And there's his Social Security card."

With a withering look, Jenkins plucked the paper from his fingers. "I know you're concerned about Miss Saylor and the Graham girl, which is why I'm not having you thrown out on your ear. But watch yourself, Hollister."

Chase gulped the words that were trying to slingshot out of his mouth. He nodded.

Jenkins studied the paper, then laid it aside. He picked up Alex's employment application and scanned it. "Didn't have much experience with candles before you hired him, did he?"

"No, but he didn't need any. Candle making isn't hard. What we mostly needed was someone willing to learn, who could pick up the slack after Kevin—" Chase couldn't bring himself to continue.

Jenkins returned the paper to the file. "I heard something from Graham a few minutes ago you might like to know. He said he's pretty sure Alex Young forced heroin on your friend before he killed him."

The room wavered. Chase placed his hands on the desk and

leaned his weight on them. *I knew it, buddy. I knew it. You weren't using drugs after all.*

He cleared his throat. "So Alex for sure killed Kevin?"

Jenkins lifted a shoulder. "Graham seemed fairly certain about that. He thinks Young approached him with the scheme to place drugs in the candles, and when Duncan refused, he killed him to keep the scheme secret. Then he took his place at your factory."

"But why would he force Kevin to take heroin?"

Jenkins shook his head. "Son, if there's one thing I've learned in this business, it's that drug dealers like Young are just plain evil. Sometimes there's no rhyme or reason to their actions, other than pure meanness."

He'd been jumping to conclusions for a year now. First Kevin, and then Korey. And he'd jumped to the wrong conclusion about Alex, too. He'd missed recognizing a cold-blooded killer, even though he worked with him day in and day out for almost a year.

Kevin, I'm sorry. I shouldn't have doubted you.

"Maybe we're wrong." An unreasonable hope swelled behind his breastbone. "What if we're jumping to conclusions, and Caitlin and Nicky are off eating an ice-cream cone somewhere? I've been wrong about a lot of things lately."

Jenkins held his eye for a long moment. "You're not wrong about this."

"How do you know?" Chase issued the question as a challenge.

The detective tapped the phone receiver. "Deputy Matthews just searched Miss Saylor's room at the Nashville Inn. He found blood on one of the beds."

The room around Chase dimmed. *If that slime bucket hurt Caitlin—*

"Not a lot," Jenkins hurried to add. "A few drops, such as

might come from a minor wound. But blood in the room of a missing woman is proof that something's amiss."

The cell phone at his belt beeped. He picked it up, glanced at the screen, and answered. "Jenkins here. What'd you find?" His lips pursed as he listened. "All right. Secure it. I don't know how long it'll be before we can spare an evidence tech. We're keeping them busy today. In the meantime, get over to the Graham residence and see if Matthews and Kincaid need any help."

He hung up the phone and heaved a sigh. "Young's apartment is clean. No drugs, no paraphernalia."

"And no hostages." Chase's voice was flat.

Jenkins shook his head.

Where are you, Caitlin? Where did he take you?

"I was sure you'd find something there. I mean, he doesn't receive the drugs already divided up in all those little tin packets. Doesn't heroin come in big plastic bags?"

"The powder form does. The stuff we're dealing with here looks more like a lump of coal. Only sticky, like hardened tar." The detective stared at the ceiling, silent a moment. "Still, you'd think it would arrive in a large quantity, and Young would have to break it up. He'd need equipment for that, scales and so on. Where did he do it?"

"Willie's place?" Chase suggested.

Jenkins shook his head. "We searched there this morning. Nothing like that on the premises. Besides, Evans was an addict. Young wouldn't trust him with that much heroin."

"Then he has another place. Someplace we don't know about." Realization dawned on Chase. "I'll bet that's where he's taken Caitlin and the girl. We just have to find out where that is."

"Did he have friends? Someone he might have talked to?"

Chase shook his head. "I have no idea who he knew outside of work. He liked to hang out in bars, that's all I know."

Jenkins shot out of the chair. "At least we have one person in custody who might know something. And he's motivated to help."

Chase trailed the detective, half-afraid he'd be ordered to leave. But he wasn't, and he stayed on Jenkins's heels all the way to the conference room where he'd been questioned earlier that afternoon. Ed Graham occupied the seat opposite the door, elbows on the table, his head in his hands. When they entered, the man looked up, hope flaring in his red-rimmed eyes.

"Have you found Nicky?" He glanced from the detective to Chase and back again.

Jenkins shook his head. "Not yet. But we're doing everything we can." The detective punched a button on the recorder, and the machine began a quiet whirr. "I need to ask you another question about Young. What do you know about his process? Did he package the heroin himself, or did it come to him prepackaged?"

"I have no idea. We never talked about that. I've never even seen heroin myself. Just the candles," Graham said.

"What about a location? Did he ever mention anything about where he went to pick up his shipments? Or maybe he mentioned a private place he liked to hang out?"

Graham sat silently a minute, chewing on his lip. "We met a couple of days before every shipment at the Moonlight Tavern for a drink. That's where I paid him for—" his gaze flickered toward Chase "—the candles. But he never mentioned anywhere else."

Chase folded his arms to keep from pummeling Graham. This guy was almost as big a slime bucket as Alex. How could Jenkins keep his temper in check while talking to him? Why didn't he get in the man's face?

The detective nodded. "Okay. We'll send someone to the Moonlight Tavern." He flicked off the recorder. "I checked with the deputy at the hospital. Your son is out of surgery."

Graham straightened. "And?"

Jenkins's voice softened. "He's okay. In serious but stable condition. The doctor says he's going to make it."

"Oh, thank goodness." Graham leaned his head backward, his eyes closed. "Thank goodness."

"There's more."

He looked up.

"Deputies searched the wreckage of the automobile he and the other boy were driving. They found two purple candles, broken into chunks."

After one frozen moment, Ed Graham collapsed across the table, sobbing as though his heart had been torn in half.

Never in a million years did Chase think he would feel sorry for a slimy drug dealer.

TWENTY

Inside the green Toyota, Caitlin clutched the seat belt and watched the road. If a miracle happened and they got away from Alex, she needed to know where they were. He'd made a couple of turns off the highway that led out of town. Left, then right. The road swelled with the land and the Toyota swerved around several wide curves. Not many cars passed them on this two-lane road, but they continued to drive by single-story houses with long front yards, tucked back from the road in deep shade from all the trees.

"So, what's wrong with your brother, kid? Why's he in the hospital?" Alex's question startled Caitlin. He actually sounded curious.

Nicky continued to stare out the passenger window. She remained silent.

Alex met Caitlin's gaze in the mirror.

"Come on, tell me what's going on. Is he sick?"

Nicky answered without turning her head. "He was in a car wreck."

"I'm sorry to hear that." He did sound sorry, the liar.

Nicky glanced at him. "You are?"

Don't talk to him, Nicky. Don't let him draw you in. He's a sick, sick person.

"Sure. But you know who I feel sorriest for?" That got the girl's full attention. "Your mom. She may lose both her kids in one day."

A choked cry came from Nicky's throat, her chest heaving.

Anger flared in Caitlin. "That's enough! You leave her alone, do you hear me? You're just being cruel." Surprised at her own temerity, she snapped her jaw shut. She'd just scolded a murderer.

Instead of flaring up, Alex laughed. "You've got spunk, I'll give you that. No wonder Chase wanted to keep you to himself."

Tears stung her eyes at the mention of Chase's name. Her watch read ten past six. In twenty minutes he would arrive at the hotel to pick her up. Surely he'd try to call when she didn't meet him in the lobby as they arranged. He'd get no answer.

Oh, Chase, hurry. When you realize we're missing, you'll look for us, I know you will.

The whole idea of the dateless year seemed ridiculous now. If she'd known what a short time she'd have with Chase, she would have thrown herself into his arms, rebound or not. The memory of their last moments together, that brief but powerful kiss on the cheek, lingered. If a miracle happened and she made it through this ordeal, she wouldn't hesitate to tell him how she felt.

Maybe someone else was searching for them by now. Janie would have remembered her daughter, no matter how distracted she was by her son's condition. Wouldn't she?

Lord, please nudge someone. Let them know we're in trouble.

The houses whizzed by outside, getting farther and farther apart, separated by thick stands of forest. She hadn't seen an oncoming car in several minutes, and very few people were in the yards they passed. Fear crept toward terror. He was taking them way back in the hills, where no one could find them. And when he got them there...

Up ahead, Caitlin caught sight of someone getting out of a car parked at the front of a long driveway. The woman left the door open while she walked toward a mailbox along the side of the road.

If only Caitlin weren't sitting in the center of the backseat. If she were near the door, she'd punch the automatic window button and scream for help as they went by. Maybe she could—

She watched the back of Alex's head as she leaned toward the door. But she was too slow. Her finger hadn't even reached the button when they zoomed past the woman.

Six-fifteen. Chase paced in front of Jenkins's desk while the detective stared at the papers in Alex's personnel folder. What did the guy hope to get out of them? And more importantly, why wasn't he *doing* something?

Chase planted his feet and glared at the man. "We can't just sit here. Every minute we waste, Alex is getting farther and farther away with them."

Jenkins set down the I-9 and returned to the employment application. For the fifth time.

"We're not just sitting here. The AMBER Alert network is in full alert mode. I have every available deputy scouring this town. There are a couple at the hotel, a team at Graham's store, and another at his house. Yet another at Young's apartment. And when Matthews is finished at the house, he's heading to the Moonlight Tavern to question everyone there. We're covering every base."

As he studied the paper, one hand tugged at the hair behind his ear. Chase fought an unreasonable impulse to reach across the desk and pull that hair out by the roots. He shoved his hands in his pockets.

"Why don't we go to the Moonlight Tavern and question people ourselves?"

Jenkins raised his eyes without moving his head. "We?"

Chase threw his hands in the air. "You can't expect me to sit around and do nothing!"

"That's exactly what I expect you to do, Hollister. You've given us everything you have that's pertinent. We appreciate your help. Now go away. Go home. Let us handle this."

He'd go crazy sitting at home. Surely Jenkins knew that. "I'll go to the Moonlight Tavern myself."

He headed toward the door, but the detective's voice stopped him. "If you do, you'll find yourself cooling your jets in a holding cell until this thing is over."

"You can't throw me in jail for no reason."

Jenkins rocked back in his chair and folded his hands across his middle. The look he fixed on Chase said, *Try me.*

Chase returned to the desk, where he stood silent and fuming.

Jenkins picked up the application and held it in front of his face, his elbow propped on the desk. "Something's bugging me about this, but I can't put my finger on it. Young worked at a convenience store in Santa Fe for two years before moving to Indiana. Prior to that, he says he was self-employed as an auto mechanic."

"Yeah, so?"

"Did you check his references?"

"Of course. Well, from his most recent job. There was nobody to call for a business he ran out of his garage." Chase closed his eyes and tried to remember. "I talked to the manager of the convenience store. Actually, he wasn't too happy with Alex. Said he'd been fairly reliable, but apparently his mother got sick and he took off with no notice other than a brief phone message."

"And you hired him anyway?"

The interview with Alex was pretty vague in Chase's mind. He'd been an emotional wreck at the time, reeling over Kevin's violent death and the allegations of his drug use. "He said his mom had been in an accident and he had to hurry to get to her before she died." Chase remembered now. He'd felt sorry for Alex at the time, and a sense of kinship with him over losing someone close unexpectedly. "After she died, he said he didn't want to go back to Santa Fe, and he couldn't force himself to stay at her place in Minnesota. So he headed east until he landed in Nashville and decided this would be a good town to call home."

"Lucky us." Jenkins stared at the paper a second more, then his eyes narrowed. "Wait a minute. New Mexico. Minnesota. Indiana. Did he ever mention living anyplace else? Like Phoenix, maybe?"

Chase shook his head. "Not that I ever heard."

"Because Graham said when he met Young, he'd just moved here from Phoenix."

Chase shrugged. "He was probably lying."

"Yeah, but to which one of you?"

What difference did it make? Chase didn't see how this conversation could help them find Caitlin and Nicky. "I don't know. Does it matter?"

"It might." Jenkins slid the computer keyboard toward him and started punching keys, his gaze fixed on the monitor. "Anything we can learn about this guy might give us a lead."

Curious in spite of the mounting sense of urgency that wouldn't let him stand still, Chase circled around to stand behind Jenkins's chair. A database appeared on the screen. Jenkins clicked the mouse and a picture of Alex popped up. The muscles in Chase's stomach clenched at the sight of the dirty rat.

"There's his current driver's license record," Jenkins commented. "We're spreading that picture around the state, along with a description of his car and the hostages."

The hostages. Chase shut his eyes against the blast of emotion that battered him. That was Caitlin he was talking about. The woman he very well might be falling in love with, as crazy as it was. And he had turned her into a hostage with a single, unwitting act.

"Let's take a look at this one online." Jenkins tapped the photocopy of Alex's New Mexico license.

The picture he pulled up on the screen didn't match the copy in Alex's personnel file. Alex was dark-haired, with an oval face and a square jaw. The blond man staring at him from the detective's screen had a long, gaunt face and protruding cheekbones. No similarity at all.

"That's not Alex."

Jenkins glanced over his shoulder at him. "I have a feeling this is the real Alexander Young."

"You mean Alex—the one we're dealing with—stole this man's identity?"

"And his car, and maybe even his life. That's why the Alex Young who was employed by that convenience store didn't quit in person."

The reason became clear to Chase. "Because he was dead."

Jenkins shrugged. "Maybe."

"But I still don't understand where Phoenix fits into the picture. If Alex, or whoever he is, came from Phoenix, what was he doing in New Mexico?"

Jenkins spoke while his fingers flew over the keyboard. "I don't want to make any assumptions at this point." He picked up the phone.

"Yes, this is Detective Mark Jenkins with the Brown County, Indiana, Sheriff's Department. We've got a kidnap-

ping situation here, and I'm trying to trace the movements of
a suspect. I think he might have roots out your way. Could you
check your records for any unsolved murders—" he picked up
the employment application and glanced at it "—let's say
from January to April last year. The guy uses a knife to slit
the vics' throats. Yes, I'll hold." Jenkins covered the receiver
with a hand and spoke over his shoulder. "Would you quit
hovering?"

Chase returned to the front of the desk. The man ought to
get another chair in here, so his visitors wouldn't wear out the
carpet pacing.

After an interminably long wait, Jenkins said, "That's the
same MO. You ID any suspects?" He caught Chase's eye, a
grim set to his mouth as he listened. "That might be our man.
Think you could send me a picture?" He gave his e-mail
address, then propped the phone up with a shoulder as he
typed.

Chase leaned across the desk and watched as Jenkins pulled
up his e-mail software. Then he grabbed the mouse and clicked
the receive button over and over, the only visible sign that he
was as impatient as Chase.

Finally. New mail. Jenkins double-clicked on it, and a
picture opened up on the screen.

A picture of Alex.

Jenkins glanced at Chase, who nodded.

"That's our man," he told the person on the phone. "He's
been here a year, and at the moment he's disappeared, along
with a woman and twelve-year-old child. If you have any case
notes to share with me, I'd sure appreciate it." Pause. "All right.
Thanks."

He slammed the phone down. "His name is Frank Edward
Adams, a mechanic at a brake-repair shop in Phoenix. He
was identified as a person of interest in the murder of a known

drug dealer last February. Guy's throat was slit. Adams disappeared before the police could bring him in for questioning."

Chase closed his eyes. "We've got to find them, Detective. Before it's too late."

Jenkins glanced at his watch, then launched himself out of the chair. "Let's go."

Chase straightened. "Where are we going?"

"The Moonlight Tavern."

"You're taking me with you?"

Jenkins eyed him as he rounded the desk. "I want you where I can keep an eye on you. Short of locking you up, this is the next best way."

TWENTY-ONE

The Toyota rounded a sharp curve and Caitlin lurched sideways, the seat belt the only thing stopping her from being thrown around the backseat. They'd left the last house behind several miles back on this deserted country road, and her hopes with it. Thick trees crowded the road on both sides. How would anyone ever find them way out here?

Lord, is somebody looking for us? Send them this way.

Even as she prayed, despair snatched at any confidence she might have mustered. She'd given up trying to figure out a way to leave a trail. If the windows had been open she could have dropped items from her purse. But apparently Alex had foreseen that possibility. They remained closed.

As far as she could see, the only chance she and Nicky had to survive this ordeal rested in trying to convince Alex to let them go.

Or at least let Nicky go.

"Alex, why don't you stop the car and let Nicky out."

The girl jerked her head around, eyes wide. Caitlin poured as much confidence into her words as she could manage.

Alex gave a single laugh. "Now why would I do that?"

"Because she's just a child. And because you don't need her. You'd still have me."

He didn't look at her. "I don't need you, either."

The implication that hung in the air left her light-headed. He was going to get rid of them.

"But wouldn't it look better for you if you let her go? I mean, crimes against children carry more severe penalties, don't they?"

"That would be a good point, if I planned to get caught." He looked at her in the mirror. "I don't."

A narrow dirt drive lay up ahead through the trees on the right. The car slowed, and Caitlin bounced as the tires left the pavement and pulled onto the path.

"That's a nice gesture, though. See, kid, she's looking out for you." He patted Nicky's knee, and the girl shrank against the door, putting as much distance as possible between her and Alex.

He laughed, unperturbed. "That's another reason Chase likes you, Caitlin. You don't mind if I call you Caitlin, do you?" He didn't wait for an answer. "You both buy in to that church baloney. 'Do unto others' and 'Love your neighbor' and all that. Personally, I think it's a load of garbage."

Caitlin didn't respond. He was goading her, bringing up Chase's name and making fun of her beliefs. Well, it wouldn't work. She refused to fall into his cruel trap.

She closed her eyes and conjured up a memory. Chase, seated close to her in the church pew, the warmth of his leg pressing against hers. Their voices blending as they sang along with the gospel band.

"I mean, come on. What do you really get out of all that church stuff?" He kept both hands on the wheel as the car bumped over the rough trail. Tree branches mingled overhead to form a rapidly darkening canopy. "It's nothing but a bunch of nonsense rules without any payoff. You don't get anything out of doing unto others."

"Of course you do." The words left Caitlin's mouth before she could stop them.

"Yeah? Like what?"

She watched his profile as she spoke. "Satisfaction in another person's happiness, for one. And if you've been kind to someone, they're eager to help you in return."

His lips tightened into a hard line. "Not always, they're not."

He's been hurt. The realization shocked Caitlin, not because she had any trouble believing Alex had lived a painful past, but because a whisper of compassion accompanied the thought.

I don't care what he's been through. Lots of people suffer terrible ordeals and they don't become murderers. They don't abduct children.

Something her pastor said once came back to her. "If the only person living in the world had been the vilest of sinners, Jesus would have still died to save him."

Lord, can You save Alex?

And was it completely selfish to pray for that to happen, because that might be the only way to save Nicky and herself?

She leaned forward and rested her forearms on her legs. "Christians don't treat others kindly because it's a rule, you know."

"Oh, yeah?" Sarcasm dripped from his tone. "Then why?"

"We're kind because God is kind. The love we have for others is an overflow of the love He has for us."

A heavy silence filled the car. The drone of the engine and a faint rattle from the air conditioner fan pressed on Caitlin's ears.

Then Alex spoke, his voice low and full of menace. "Lady, I have killed five people without blinking an eye, two of them within the past three days. If you want to live another sixty seconds, you'll shut your mouth and keep it shut."

Caitlin gulped down the fear that rose like acid in her throat. She sat up slowly and pressed herself into the seat back while Nicky huddled against the door.

Five people? He'd already admitted to murdering Willie, and no doubt Lancaster, the man Chase had found in the park. That meant he'd probably killed Kevin last year, too, and two more, besides. If only she could tell Chase. It might help him to know for sure who was responsible for his friend's death.

And if she couldn't get away soon, for hers, as well.

The bumpy dirt trail ended in a clearing. Alex stopped the car in front of a run-down cabin. The lone window on this side of the building had eight panes, the glass missing in two of them. Moss grew in patches on the dilapidated roof.

He turned the ignition off. "We're here."

The chill in his words snatched the breath from Caitlin's lungs.

It can't end like this. Not here, not now. There's too much to live for. Jazzy. Liz. My music. My faith. My... Chase.

No. It can't end like this.

TWENTY-TWO

Gray ribbons of smoke rose from a dozen ashtrays inside the Moonlight Tavern. Chase's lungs revolted when he stepped through the door, and he exploded in a coughing fit. He stopped just over the threshold to catch his breath. When he had control of himself, he looked up to find every face in the room turned his way. Most did not look friendly.

Jenkins turned to face him, eyes rolling in disgust.

"What?" Chase asked, his voice low. "Cigarette smoke makes me cough."

"Then maybe you'd better wait in the car."

He drew in a shuddering breath and held back another cough. "I can handle it."

Jenkins held his gaze for a long moment, then shook his head. "Just keep quiet. I'll do the talking." He made his way to the bar, a giant half-circle slab of varnished dark wood that dominated half of the tavern. A flat-screen television showed a baseball game at one end of the bar. To the right, three men stood around a pool table with cue sticks while a fourth leaned over the table to take a difficult shot.

Chase followed the detective and slid onto a bar stool next to him. Across the way a man lifted a mug of beer with unsteady hands and sloshed it down his shirt when he tried to gulp from it. Six-thirty on a Thursday night, and he was already drunk. A woman two stools to the man's right sat with her elbows on the bar and watched Chase over the rim of a glass with a lemon floating in it. He looked away from her loaded gaze. The man on the other side of Jenkins sucked hard on a cigarette and eyed Chase as he blew a cloud of smoke in his direction.

Nice.

The bartender, a burly man with a head the shape of a basketball, took his own sweet time sauntering over to their end of the bar. "What can I get for you gentlemen?"

"Just some information, if you don't mind." Jenkins produced a copy of Alex's Indiana driver's license photo. "I understand this man comes in here fairly often."

The bartender picked up the paper, studied it, then dropped it back on the bar and slid it toward the detective with a finger. "Don't know his last name. First name's Alex."

"That's him. What can you tell me about him?"

The bartender shook his head. "Not much. Comes in here two, three times a week. Keeps pretty much to himself. Has a couple of drinks. Leaves. Usually alone."

Jenkins's eyebrows arched. "Usually?"

The man jerked his head once toward the woman across the bar. "You might ask Pat what she knows about him." He smirked. "They've talked a few times." He lifted his head in the direction of the woman. "Hey, Pat, these gentlemen would like to have a word with you."

Her lips curved into a slow smile as she slid off the stool, picked up her drink, and came around the bar toward them. As she came fully into view, Chase saw that she wasn't shy about showing off her assets, so to speak. She selected the empty stool next to him, and he made a point of not looking at the expanse of thigh showing beneath a skirt half the size it should have been.

"How can I help you?" Her gaze slid sideways toward Chase, a half smile playing around her lips.

Chase cleared his throat and looked at Jenkins. He was supposed to be driving this interrogation, wasn't he?

Jenkins slid the picture across the bar. "I understand you know this man."

She picked it up. The flirty smile faded. "Yeah, I do. Alex Young. We've gone out a few times." She held on to the picture, staring into Alex's face with an unreadable expression. "What's he done?"

"Maybe nothing." Jenkins pulled the paper gently from her fingers. "Maybe something really bad. What can you tell us about him?"

"Not much. He's a pretty closed guy, you know?" She sipped from her glass. Ice tinkled as she set it on the bar.

"What do you mean, closed?"

Her finger trailed the rim of the glass. "He's great looking, and fun on a date, but you can't get anything out of him. Nothing personal." She wet her lips and flashed a quick glance at Chase. "Whenever I tried to talk to him, ask him about his family or something, he clammed up."

That sounded like Alex. Though he'd joined the company a year ago, Chase knew almost nothing about his personal life. He never spoke of his family. Chase had assumed it was because his mother's death was still too fresh, too raw.

"Where did he spend his time?"

"He worked at that candle factory out on Old Soldier's Lane. You know the one?" Her gaze took in Chase and Jenkins both. Chase nodded. "Didn't seem to like the job much. Said one of his bosses didn't do anything, left all the work to him. The other was a do-gooder. Alex didn't have much use for him."

Chase clenched his teeth. The jerk.

"What about outside of work? Did he talk about his hobbies, where he liked to hang out?" Jenkins's head swiveled as he looked around the bar. "Other than here."

The woman's gaze became distant as she picked up her glass. Then her face cleared. "Yeah, he liked to hunt. Last November he told me he saw a bunch of deer in the woods near some cabin. He was thinking about getting a deer tag."

A cabin. Chase exchanged a look with Jenkins.

"Did he say where the cabin was?" How the detective kept so calm was beyond Chase. The woman started to shake her head, but he went on. "Think hard. It's important."

Jenkins raised his eyes to the television screen at the end of the bar. The woman twisted around on the bar stool and followed his gaze. So did Chase. The local news station had broken into the ballgame with an AMBER Alert announcement. The volume was too low to hear, but a description of the alert scrolled across the bottom of the screen. Then the picture changed to a close-up of Nicky's face. A moment later, the picture changed again, and Caitlin's clear gaze, taken from the Kentucky drivers' license online database, stared into Chase's.

Pain punched him in the gut.

Oh, Caitlin. I'm so sorry I got you into this mess. If anything happens to you...

The picture on the screen changed once again. Alex. Or rather, Frank Edward Adams.

The woman jerked back toward them, her face ashen.

Jenkins spoke in that same calm tone. "Now you see why we need to find him quickly."

She gulped. "He didn't say where that cabin was, only that it was in the woods. And he only mentioned it that one time. Never again." She turned a beseeching gaze on Chase. "Honest. If I knew anything, I'd tell you."

"I'm sure you would." Jenkins slid off his stool, and placed a card on the bar in front of her. "In case you remember anything that might be helpful."

Her fingers trembled as she picked it up. She was still staring at it when they left the bar.

The clean air tasted sweet in the back of Chase's throat. "At least we got a lead." He went to the passenger side of Jenkins's cruiser.

"A cabin in the woods." The detective unlocked the driver's door. "Do you know how many miles of woods surround this area? We could search all day, every day, for a solid month and still not cover it all."

"We could call in the public." Nashville was a caring community. They'd come out by the hundreds to comb through every acre of woods until they found Caitlin and Nicky.

Jenkins opened his door, then stood with his arm across the frame. "We will. But it will take several hours to assemble that kind of search party. And it'll be dark soon. It's too dangerous to have civilians wandering the woods at night." He ducked into the car.

Chase's shoulders slumped. Jenkins was right. A full-scale search like that couldn't get into swing until first light. And that may be too late.

The phone in his pocket rang. He ignored it and slid into the passenger seat.

"You going to get that?"

Chase shook his head. It was probably his mom or Korey calling to get an update. He was too glum to talk to anybody right now.

"It might be important."

Fine. Chase heaved a sigh as he slipped his cell out. "Hello?"

"Chase Hollister, what did you do to that girl?"

A familiar voice. It took a moment to register. "Maude?"

"I saw that pretty girl, Caitlin, out my way a while back

when I was checking the mail. Something wasn't right. Did you upset her?"

Chase jerked upright. "You saw Caitlin?"

Jenkins turned to look at him.

"I'm sure it was her. Now, I know the Lord doesn't like a busybody, but I just couldn't get her out of my mind. So I looked up your number in the church directory. Now listen, I know your mama would like to see you fixed up with a nice Christian girl like—"

"Maude!" Chase's heart slammed against his ribcage. "Haven't you been watching television?"

"Why, no. I don't turn that thing on at night. Peace and quiet, that's what I like around my place of an evening."

A choke gurgled in Chase's throat. "Maude, Caitlin has been kidnapped, along with a twelve-year-old girl. The whole state is looking for them. Where did you see her?"

"Kidnapped?" A gasp. Her voice rose to a shout. "Why, I saw them. They were right here on my road. There was a girl in the front seat beside the man, and your sweetie was in the back. No wonder she looked upset."

"Where, Maude?" Chase pounded the dashboard with every word. "Where did you see them?"

"Out here on Mackenzie Pike. They were in a green car, heading back into the woods." A sob strangled her words. "Oh, honey. There's a lot of woods up there."

At least it was a start. Chase looked at Jenkins. "Mackenzie Pike."

Their tires squealed as they tore out of the parking lot. Jenkins was shouting orders into his phone before they turned onto the road.

"Thank you, Maude. Thank you for being a busybody."

"What can I do? How can I help?"

"Pray." Chase closed his eyes. "Pray hard."

TWENTY-THREE

"Come on. Get out."

Caitlin fumbled for the seat belt release. Fear made her fingers awkward. How many minutes did they have left to live? She couldn't stop looking at her watch. What time would be recorded on her death certificate? By the time they found her body in this deserted location, how closely would they be able to pinpoint the exact moment she drew her last breath?

Stop it! Going all morbid isn't going to help.

But try though she might, she couldn't think of anything that *would* help.

She found the button. The buckle released, and she slid across the seat to the door Alex had opened. The tendons in his left hand bulged as he gripped Nicky's arm, the gun still clutched in his right. Terror had bleached the girl's skin a pasty white. One side of her mouth had swollen into a painful-looking grimace. She wouldn't be able to play her flute for at least a week with that injury.

Nausea swirled in Caitlin's stomach. If Alex had his way, Nicky would never play her flute again.

The knife lay open beneath her purse in the seat beside her. She should have picked it up while they were driving and slipped it into her pocket. Now Alex's glare burned into her and she didn't dare make a move for it. And even if she managed to get it without him seeing, would she use it? Could she?

Thou shalt not kill.

"Hurry up." His voice snapped with impatience.

Caitlin twisted as she slid across the seat and turned her back toward the door. Her body shielded the interior of the car for no more than three seconds. Thunder from her heart filled her ears as she slid the knife from beneath the cover of her purse. She held the plastic case in her palm. The blade nestled against the soft skin of her wrist as she climbed out of the car.

Lord, don't let him look at my hand.

The sinking sun glittered through the tops of the trees to the west of the cabin. Birds called to one another across the clearing, oblivious to the palpable terror beneath them. A squirrel scolded nearby as Caitlin closed the car door and turned to face her captor.

"Inside." His head jerked toward the cabin.

Caitlin preceded him, thoughts racing through her mind. If she was going to use her only weapon, she had to do it now. Every second that ticked by increased the chance that he would see it. And he probably planned to kill them as soon as he got them inside. But she couldn't do anything as long as he had that gun pressed into Nicky's side.

The door's scarred surface had never been painted. Slender gaps riddled the splintered wood.

"Go ahead. There's no lock."

The door swung inward. Caitlin stepped up onto the thick, uneven plank floor. The gloom of dusk had settled inside the cabin. The air smelled dusty and dank. Little sunlight shone through the filthy window panes, but there was enough to make out an ancient-looking counter along the back wall and a folding table with one metal chair. A metal clasp had been hooked between the handles of the two cabinet doors, secured with a padlock. The room contained nothing else. The heels of her sandals returned a hollow echo from the rough plank walls.

Caitlin stopped in the center of the room and turned. She didn't dare clutch at the knife for fear he'd see she held something hidden in her hand. Instead, she held the case in place with light pressure from her thumb, her fingers curved in a natural pose. She hoped.

Alex closed the door.

"Well, this is it." His glance circled the room, then came to rest on her with a tight smile. "I admit it isn't much, but it has a couple of good points." He pulled Nicky around the perimeter of the room, watching Caitlin as he moved. "It's owned by the father of a friend of mine from California, a man who's too old to use it anymore, and it's out in the middle of nowhere, away from prying eyes."

Caitlin's mind raced. Is this where he'd killed some of his victims? Acid burned the back of her throat. She covered her mouth as she scanned the wood floor for signs of violence.

"Since you're here, you two might as well make yourselves useful. It seems I have to vacate the premises, and there are a few things I'd rather not leave behind. They'll come in handy when I settle somewhere else."

He approached the counter. As he moved, he released Nicky with a shove.

Caitlin's heart stuttered. Was this her chance?

Suddenly freed from her captor's grip, a sobbing Nicky launched herself across the room toward Caitlin, arms flung wide. They collided with unexpected force. Time crashed to a halt.

The knife flew from Caitlin's palm.

Her only hope for survival skittered across the floor. The

quiet thud as it smacked the door was her death knell. Horror spread over Caitlin like a stain. Alex looked at the knife. Then he fixed a glittering glare on her.

He crossed the room in three strides, his arm cocked back. "You stupid—"

The rest of his sentence was swallowed up in blackness as his fist connected with her face.

TWENTY-FOUR

Red and blue lights stuttered against the trees and flashed in Chase's eyes. A half dozen police vehicles lined the highway at the intersection to Mackenzie Pike, four from the sheriff's department and two belonging to the state police. Two more formed a V across the road to prevent anyone from entering or leaving.

"All right, listen up." Detective Jenkins spread a map out on the hood of his car.

Chase itched to elbow his way into the group, but he didn't dare. Any minute someone might voice a complaint about the civilian and Jenkins would send him packing. There was no way they were kicking him out now. They'd have to haul him off in handcuffs.

"Here's Mackenzie Pike." Jenkins's finger traced a line on the map. Chase angled sideways so he could see between two deputies. "If our information is right, Adams is somewhere in this area." His finger traced a circle on the map.

"That's a lot of land to cover," said one of the deputies.

Chase traced Mackenzie Pike in his mind. Probably twenty miles of twisting country road through mostly unpopulated and heavily forested hill country. He fought against the tug of despair. Even with four times as many police officers, it would take hours and hours to search all that land.

"Yes, it is. But remember, he may be holed up in a cabin, and he's in a car, not on foot, so look in every garage and search every trail big enough for a vehicle to pass. We'll start right here, where Adams's car was spotted, and work our way inside. Stop at every house. Those starting at the other end will do the same." He glanced up at the flashing light bar atop the cruiser. "No sirens or lights. Let's try to take him by surprise."

Chase pressed himself against the car door as the officers surged past him toward their cruisers.

"Get in," Jenkins said.

"Where are we going?"

"I want to get an official statement from your friend. See if she knows anything else that might help."

Chase jerked the car door open. Maude was the last person to see Caitlin and Nicky—he stopped himself from finishing the sentence. He refused to consider that she might have been the last to see Caitlin alive.

God, You know I don't ask much. But this is my fault, and I can't stand the thought of... He swallowed against a tight throat. *Just lead us to them, please. Let us find them in time.*

One of the state police vehicles blocking the road moved aside to let the searchers through. Jenkins followed. When they'd gone by, Chase turned to watch the roadblock close up behind them. No one was getting through that way.

Maude's place lay about four miles up Mackenzie Pike on the left. Lights glowed in the windows of the sprawling, single-story brick home. When Jenkins's car pulled down the dirt driveway, the front door flew open.

"That's her."

Maude leaned heavily on the railing to climb down three steps from her front stoop, but the minute her feet touched the grass she raced toward them. Chase got out of the car and found himself engulfed in a tight embrace.

"Oh, honey, I haven't gotten off my knees since we hung up." She backed up and wrung her hands. "I'm just sick. I had my car right there. I should have jumped in and followed them, seen where they went."

"Don't do this to yourself, Maude." Chase covered her hands with his. "You've helped more than anyone. Because of you, we still have a chance to find them."

"He's right, ma'am," Jenkins said. "And now, if you don't mind, I'd like you to tell me exactly what you saw."

She nodded and closed her eyes. "I was just coming home from work. I stopped for the mail like I always do. Right over there." She pointed toward the front of the driveway.

"What time was that?" Chase asked.

She replied without hesitation. "Six-fifteen. Same time as every other day, except the Lord's Day. I was standing there glancing through the mail when a car came down the road."

"Did you notice the make and model?" asked Jenkins.

Worry lines creased her brown forehead. "I don't know a Chevy from a Ford. I just know it was green and shaped like a box. You know, not a sporty car. Just the regular kind. It did have four doors."

Chase squeezed her hand. Alex's Toyota was green and had four doors.

"That's all right." Jenkins smiled. "Go on."

Maude relayed the same information she'd told Chase on the phone, that she'd recognized Caitlin in the backseat, and that she looked upset.

"How do you know she was upset?" Jenkins prodded.

Maude's brows crouched low over her eyes. "I don't know. She just was. She wasn't smiling like every other time I've seen her."

Caitlin's smile rose unbidden in Chase's mind. Would he ever see it again?

"And besides, the Lord stirred my soul." Maude's chin jutted out, daring them to doubt her. "Say what you want, but I know He did. He wouldn't let me get that girl off my mind until I called Chase."

Detective Jenkins twisted on his heel and stared up the road, in the direction Maude had seen the Toyota drive. "Is there any place up there where someone could hide out? We got word that he may be holed up in a cabin somewhere."

"Oh, honey, there's a bunch of cabins in these woods." She waved a hand. "During deer season this place is packed with hunters. It isn't safe to walk in your own front yard without covering yourself head to toe in orange."

"A deserted cabin, maybe?" Chase asked. "He wouldn't use one where the owner might find him. He'd want someplace where there was no chance of a surprise visit."

Maude tilted her head. "You know, there is old Mr. Owens's place about three, four miles up the road. He hasn't been up there in more than ten years, not since he moved to the nursing home. His kids all live out west somewhere, so they don't ever go up there."

Jenkins's expression did not change, but the intensity in his eyes stirred up an excitement in Chase. This could be it.

"How do I get there?" Jenkins was already rounding his car as he asked the question.

Maude pointed. "Head that way and look for a path off to the right." She hesitated. "There isn't a sign or anything."

Chase's blood raced through his veins. Finally, they were getting somewhere. He jerked open the car door.

"Where do you think you're going?" Jenkins demanded.

Chase stopped. "I'm going with you."

"No, you're not." The detective's jaw took on a stubborn set. "You're going to stay right here and wait."

Chase slapped a hand on the roof. "I can't stay here. You need every able-bodied man you can get. I can help."

Jenkins pierced him with a stare. "Do you really want to waste my time arguing over this?"

Seconds ticked by as Chase glared at the detective. Seconds that might mean the difference between life and death for Caitlin.

He took out his frustration on the door. It slammed shut with a thud that rattled the windows. Knots formed in Chase's insides as the detective's car backed out of the driveway and disappeared around a bend in the road.

Maude looked intently at Chase.

"Not too many years ago, when my daddy was still living, he and old Mr. Owens used to hunt together. Deer, squirrel, rabbit. Whatever was in season." She put her hand on her hip. "And sometimes, whatever wasn't in season, truth be told."

Chase did not have time to listen to the woman's reminiscing. Here he stood, doing nothing while Caitlin and Nicky were in mortal danger at the hands of a cold-blooded killer. Thanks to him.

"He had him a shortcut, a path right through the woods. It's at least four miles between here and there by road, but not more than half a mile on that path, I'd say." She pointed across the street. "Right over there."

It took a moment for Chase to process the information she'd just given him. Then he whirled toward her. "Do you think the path is still there?"

She squinted her eyes in that direction. "This end's still there. See it? Right between those two trees."

Chase didn't waste time. He dashed across the road, aiming for the opening in the trees she'd pointed out.

Maude's voice called out after him. "Chase Hollister, you be careful, you hear me?"

As he slipped into the trees, he turned his head and shouted, "I will! Keep praying!"

TWENTY-FIVE

Chase's arms folded Caitlin in a warm embrace.

"I thought I'd never see you again." Her words were muffled by his shirt as she snuggled close. "I was afraid I'd never get to tell you how I felt."

His voice rumbled in his chest. "Tell me now."

She closed her eyes. "I know we just met, but—"

"Wake up. Please wake up."

Nicky's tearful voice urged Caitlin to consciousness.

Oh, Lord! Let me stay in the dream!

The intense throbbing in her head was proof enough that this nightmare was real. The effort she exerted to open her eyes sent shafts of pain through her head. Her left eye cooperated. A weight pressed against the right one. Swelling had already begun.

How long was I out?

Nicky's anxious face swam into view. "You're awake. I thought you were going to die."

I am. We both are. Don't you know that?

Alex's voice grated on her ears like an obscenity. "Finally awake, is she?"

Hammers pounded in her head. The temptation to sink back into oblivion was almost overwhelming. But she couldn't leave Nicky to face the monster alone.

"About time you woke up." His face appeared behind Nicky's. "I've almost finished up here. Almost time for me to hit the road."

She became aware of details. The rough, bare floor beneath her. Faint strains of a country music song. Her feet crossed at the ankles. One shoe missing. Pain radiating from the back of her head as well as her temple and eye ridge. Apparently the force of his blow had knocked her backward, and she'd struck her head on the floor.

She struggled to sit up. Nicky slipped an arm behind her and helped her to a sitting position. She leaned heavily against the wall as black spots swirled in her vision and nausea almost overpowered her. Did she have a concussion?

What does it matter? I'm going to die soon anyway.

Her thoughts felt oddly detached. What did a little pain matter? It would all be over soon. She'd be in the arms of Jesus. He'd stop the pounding in her head, still the queasiness in her stomach.

But what about Nicky?

Caitlin forced herself to focus on the girl, the room.

The killer.

He stood a few feet away, watching her with an amused grin. What was that in his hands? It looked like a set of scales. Just like the ones in the chemistry lab at school. Of course. He'd need that to weigh the drugs he put inside those horrible candles. Where was the gun?

He noticed her staring at the scales. "No sense leaving perfectly good equipment behind. I'd just have to find more when I get settled somewhere else."

When he turned and left the cabin, Caitlin caught sight of the gun. He'd tucked it in the waistband of his jeans, above his right hip pocket.

Once he stepped outside, she whispered. "What's he doing?"

Nicky squatted beside her. "Loading everything from that cabinet into his car. He made me carry out a cardboard box with a roll of foil and a cutting board and some other stuff."

Caitlin touched the back of her head with hesitant fingers. It felt like half a golf ball back there. Nothing sticky, though. The music changed to a different country western song. She followed the sound to its source. A small boom box rested on the counter.

"What are we going to do?" Nicky's whisper quivered, but her grip on Caitlin's arm tightened with urgency.

Caitlin couldn't bear the trust she saw in the girl's face. How could she still expect Caitlin to save them? Her single effort had proved as futile as she'd known it would be. She couldn't even manage to move without wanting to throw up.

Lord, I'm out of ideas. Is this the end?

Caitlin shook her head and ignored the pain the movement caused. "I don't know, Nicky. I can't think straight."

The sound of a trunk shutting warned them of Alex's return. When he appeared in the doorway, Caitlin's heart slammed to a halt in her chest.

He held a knife.

Its deadly blade was longer than his hand and came to a menacing point. His fingers curved around the black plastic handle. He paused in the doorway, his expression grim. Helplessness drained the last drops of courage Caitlin had managed to hang on to. Reckless anger she could deal with. The calm purpose apparent in his stare sent terror through her.

He hefted the weapon in his hand. "As I said before, a gun isn't my preferred weapon. It's good in a pinch, but it's too noisy, and easily traceable. Not this baby, though." His grip tightened. "You can buy them at any store that sells hunting equipment."

"Alex, listen to me." Caitlin struggled to stand. Nicky wedged a shoulder beneath her arm, and she leaned heavily on it. "You don't have to do this. They're going to come after you. Killing us won't stop that."

He stepped into the room, and pulled the door closed behind him. Caitlin blinked in the remaining gloom. She could no longer see his face clearly.

"There's nothing here to tie you up with. You'll have them on my trail the minute I'm out of sight."

"We won't. We promise." Beside her, Nicky nodded with vigor. "We'll stay right here until morning. That will give you plenty of time to get far away."

"What makes you think I would be stupid enough to trust you after the stunt you pulled? You were hiding a knife." He laughed. "A toy knife, but still."

"You can trust me. Just tell us how long you want us to stay here and we will."

He took a step toward them. Caitlin and Nicky shrank back against the wall.

"I don't trust anyone."

No, he wouldn't. Trust wasn't something he understood.

A piercing tone sliced through the tension in the cabin. The sound of the Emergency Alert System.

Alex crossed to the boom box and cranked up the volume.

"The Indiana State Police have issued an AMBER Alert for a missing twelve-year-old Nashville girl. Nicole Graham was last seen at Nashville Middle School around four o'clock this afternoon in the company of Caitlin Leigh Saylor, a Kentucky resident who is also believed to have been abducted. The suspected abductor is Frank Edward Adams, known locally as Alex Young, a thirty-five-year-old white male, five feet eleven inches tall and weighing around one hundred-eighty pounds. Adams was last seen driving—"

Alex switched the power off. The hiss of his breath was the only sound in the cabin.

"Well, that changes my plans."

Nicky's arm tightened around Caitlin's middle. "You're not going to kill us?"

"Not those plans." His eyes were black holes in his face. "I'm afraid I still have to do that."

Chase followed an overgrown path that might as well have been invisible. He ran when he could, and slowed only when the faint trail between the trees became impassable. When fallen trees blocked his way, he scrambled across or around them.

How long did it take to run half a mile? Not long on the open road, maybe five minutes. But here, he lost precious time dodging under low-slung branches and hopping over dead logs. He scanned the darkening landscape around him, hoping to catch a glimpse of the deserted cabin.

And what am I going to do when I find it?

He should have asked Maude if she still had any of her father's guns. But no, he'd charged off like a fool, without a thought. His pounding heart sent blood thundering in his ears, more from nerves than exertion. He'd figure out what to do when he got there. The important thing was to find Caitlin and Nicky as soon as possible.

A slight lightening in the gloom ahead alerted him to the presence of the clearing. The sun was no longer visible, but clouds in the western sky were still pink and shed enough light to see clearly. Chase crashed to a halt just inside the tree line and stood sideways behind the thickest trunk.

Alex's Toyota was parked in front of a small, run-down cabin. No light shone through the single window beside the closed front door. What was that noise? He strained his ears beyond the chorus of crickets that filled the night. A man's voice. Impossible to make out the words from this distance.

If he were smart, he'd retreat to a safe distance and call Detective Jenkins. But every beat of his heart whispered, *Hurry! Hurry! Hurry!* If Caitlin and Nicky were still alive in there—he gulped—every second mattered.

Grass grew in the clearing, mostly uncluttered with the dead leaves that had covered the path. Chase crouched low and placed each step carefully. No noise. Silent. His breath sounded louder than his feet on the ground. He forced himself to take deep, silent breaths. The car provided a temporary place to stop and strain his ears once more. Yes, that was definitely Alex's voice. He still couldn't make out the words, but the tone and timbre were familiar. A female voice answered.

Caitlin.

The sound of her voice set off a cascade of emotions that loosened his tense muscles. He almost collapsed to the ground. Until this moment, he hadn't dared to hope. But now, knowing she was just a few yards away, he realized he'd do anything—*anything*—to hold her in his arms. Now, how to get inside and rescue her without a single weapon and no plan?

Chase slipped around the back of the Toyota and made his way to the window.

TWENTY-SIX

"You don't have to kill us, Alex." Caitlin's arm tightened around Nicky. "At least let Nicky go. She's only a child. Please, show some compassion and let her live."

Alex advanced to the center of the room. Caitlin forced herself to ignore the knife and watch his face. His features weren't clear, but maybe he could see the pleading on her face. She would get down on her knees and beg if she thought it would save Nicky.

I'm ready, Lord. I know when I die I'm going to step out of this body and into Your arms. But save Nicky from this vile monster.

An echo of her pastor's voice rang in her head. *If the only living person in the world had been the vilest of sinners...*

Her mind grappled with the thought. This man standing before her, ready to take her life and that of this innocent child, was vile, horrible, thoroughly detestable.

And Jesus loved him.

Strength poured into her quivering limbs. She may only have minutes left to live. But she could use those last minutes trying to save a life. Maybe even two.

She turned and gathered Nicky into a close embrace. She pressed her lips into the girl's hair and whispered, "When he goes for me, run."

Then she straightened and faced her killer. "Alex, listen to me. I don't know what's happened to bring you to this. It doesn't matter now. But I want you to know one thing before you kill me." She gently disentangled herself from Nicky's grasp and took a step toward him. "Jesus loves you."

He threw back his head, his harsh laugh bouncing off the walls. "Well, I have to say, that's a new approach. I've had them beg me not to kill them, but I've never had someone try to convert me to save themselves."

Caitlin shook her head. "No, I mean it. If you kill me, He'll still love you. He loves you even though He knows all about you. In fact, He knows more about you than you know yourself. The bible says He knew you when you were still in your mother's womb."

Even in the dim light, she saw his muscles tense with anger.

Chase crawled toward the cabin. His ears strained to make out the words. He felt exposed as he crept across the fifteen feet between the Toyota and the relative cover of the cabin. When he reached it, he crouched low beneath the window. A couple of panes had been broken out long ago. The voices inside carried clearly through them.

Maybe not that clearly. He blinked. Did Caitlin just tell Alex that Jesus loved him?

With painstaking care, Chase inched himself upward. His legs shook with the effort. He peeked through the window. Alex stood with his back toward Chase. Caitlin and the girl stood opposite him, their faces blocked from view. Alex held something in his hand. A weapon, no doubt.

A harsh blast of derisive laughter startled Chase. Instinctively, he crouched low to the ground. Every nerve zinged with pent-up energy as he surveyed his surroundings. The door was held closed with a latch. From this side, there didn't appear to be a lock. No telling what was on the inside, though. But if he were able to crash through, what would he do? Attack Alex with his bare hands?

Maybe there was something he could use in the car. A tire iron, a screwdriver. Anything.

He started to creep toward it, when Caitlin spoke again. Her words shocked him into immobility.

"It is not too late for you, Alex. You can still be saved." Caitlin clasped her hands in front of her and tried to ignore the way they shook. "All that emptiness inside you can go away. The pain. The guilt. The shame. You can be rid of it all. He will take it away, if you'll let Him."

"Lady, you're the one who needs saving, not me."

But she heard something in his voice that hadn't been there a minute before. An uncertainty that sent her hopes soaring.

"You're wrong. We all need saving. Every one of us. And all we have to do is ask. Ask Him to come into your heart, to fill the empty places. He wants you to ask, Alex. He's waiting for you."

What is she doing?

Chase couldn't believe his ears. Was Caitlin actually trying to *convert* Alex? A kidnapping, drug-dealing murderer?

She's lost all hope. It's her last-ditch effort to try to convince him to let them go.

And yet, a note of emotion resounded in Chase's ears. Not fear. Not entreaty or pleading, as he would certainly have understood. No, she spoke with passion. Intensity. A quiet certainty that could not be feigned.

Admiration welled up in his throat and threatened to rob him of breath. Admiration...and something else. Caitlin might just be the most remarkable woman he'd ever known. And he loved her. The realization hit him like a riptide, sucked him under.

He loved her!

For one moment, Caitlin thought she had gotten through to him. Alex hesitated, the dark pits of his eyes fixed intently on her. Her frantic prayers at that moment could find no other expression than *please, please, please!*

She knew the moment he rejected the truth. Instead of crumpling in submission, his body seemed to expand, to grow taller with purpose. In that moment she knew she had failed.

She had seconds to live. And she would not die quietly.

Lord, get Nicky out of here.

"Nicky, *run!*"

She shouted her command as loud as she could, and then followed it with a bellow that would have made Rambo proud. For the briefest of seconds, Alex was startled into inactivity.

Instinct took over. Caitlin lowered her head and charged. Yes, she might run headfirst into the knife, but her death would buy Nicky precious seconds to escape.

Instead of a sharp blade, the top of her head sank into Alex's stomach. The force of the collision propelled them both several feet across the floor. Alex lost his footing and went crashing down. Caitlin caught herself before she tumbled after.

Alex hit the floor with an audible "Umph." Something heavy skittered across the floor.

The gun.

Caitlin dove for it. The weight of the thing felt awkward in her hands. How did her fingers know where to go? With no effort at all, her pointer finger slipped onto the trigger.

She turned to find Nicky staring at her, frozen. The girl's

mouth stood open. Then she remembered Caitlin's shouted order. She swiveled toward the door.

Too late.

Alex had staggered to his feet. He lurched toward Nicky, the knife still gripped in his fist.

Caitlin pointed the gun at him.

Thou shalt not kill.

Agony ripped through her. How could she take a life? She closed her eyes.

TWENTY-SEVEN

"Nicky, *run!*"

Chase's legs, taught as loaded springs, froze as time crashed to a halt. Caitlin's yell echoed around the clearing at the same instant a movement at the treeline drew his attention.

Detective Jenkins, flanked on either side by Kincaid and Matthews. The fury in the detective's face could be clearly seen, even at this distance. In a corner of Chase's brain, he knew he'd probably end up in jail for this. But if he managed to rescue Caitlin, it would be worth time behind bars.

A gunshot cracked through the clearing.

He leaped for the door. At the same moment his hand grabbed the latch, he threw his shoulder against the wood. The door flew open and hit the wall.

He didn't have time to register the scene in the cabin before something slammed into him. He stumbled backward as the girl, Nicky, pushed past him. Her hysterical crying drowned out all other sounds until she was outside. Chase let her go and ran in.

Alex lay in the middle of the floor, a dark stain spreading across the center of his white shirt. Caitlin knelt over him, repeating something over and over. It took Chase a moment to make out her words. When he did, his heart gave an odd wrench at the intensity of her plea.

"Please don't die, Alex," she sobbed. "Please, please don't die."

"It's okay, baby. You're safe now. It's over."

The voice that had comforted her in her dream penetrated her weeping. Caitlin felt herself lifted away from Alex by strong arms. She turned instinctively and buried her face in Chase's chest.

"You came for me." Relief wilted her knees. She would have fallen if not for his embrace. "I thought I'd never see you again, but you came for me." Her words broke on a sob.

"Shhh. Don't cry." He crushed her to him. "Of course I came for you. I love you."

Her thoughts whirled. Behind her, police officers swarmed around the room and Detective Jenkins's voice shouted for an ambulance. Somewhere outside, she could hear Nicky's relieved crying. But all those things faded into the distance as Chase's words penetrated the torrent in her mind.

Did he just say...

She pulled away so she could see his face. "You do?"

He didn't have to say it again. His eyes told her everything she wanted to know. Joy swelled in her heart. Who cared about whether or not she was on the rebound? The man she loved loved her, too.

TWENTY-EIGHT

The final song of the rehearsal came to an end. Caitlin lowered her flute and looked toward the back of the sanctuary, to the three people who'd sat silently through several run-throughs of tomorrow's ceremony. Chase wore a wide smile, and raised his hands to applaud silently. Beside him, Nicky gave her two enthusiastic thumbs-up. Janie smiled, though even from here Caitlin could see the worry lines carved deep into her brow. At least both her children had survived their ordeals. And Detective Jenkins told Caitlin this morning that Ed Graham was eager to work with the police to stamp out the drug business in Little Nashville. In return, the district attorney would recommend a light sentence to the judge at his trial.

Alex's wounds, though serious, had not been fatal. Caitlin's blind shot had punctured his lung, but a surgeon had repaired the injury, thank goodness. In a few months, he'd be well enough to stand trial for a lengthy list of charges police in several states were compiling.

Caitlin thanked their audience with a grin as she twisted the mouthpiece off her flute. When she bent to stow it in her case, blood rushed to her head and threatened to set off the dreadful throbbing again. Thankfully, it faded when she straightened and a full-fledged ache didn't materialize.

"Not bad, girls." Jazzy kept her voice low so as not to interrupt the final instructions to the wedding party from the coordinator. "I think our last performance is going to be our best ever, even though one of us looks like she just went ten rounds with the heavyweight champ."

Liz smiled ruefully. "Actually, she looks like she got knocked out in the first round."

"Gee, thanks." Caitlin gingerly touched her tender eye. The swelling had gone down a little, but the spectacular blues and purples were just starting to peak. At least when she got checked over at the hospital last night they said there had been no concussion. "It's a wonder the bride didn't cancel our contract. Some of the bridezillas we've dealt with in the past couple of years wouldn't want a black-and-blue musician to spoil their beautiful wedding."

Liz laid a hand on her arm. "Well, don't be surprised if we're not included in too many of the wedding photos."

"Yeah," said Jazzy. "It's a shame you don't play the tuba. Then you could hide behind your instrument."

Caitlin swatted her playfully with a piece of sheet music. She loved this banter with her friends. It was one of the things she was going to miss when they'd both married and moved away.

When the coordinator dismissed everyone, the small group in the back of the sanctuary hurried down the aisle. Nicky hurtled herself into Caitlin's arms.

"That was awesome! You are so good. I wish I could play like you."

"You can." Caitlin returned her hug. "Just keep practicing, and one day you'll be better than me."

"Not unless I can find another really good flute teacher." She stepped back and examined Caitlin's face. "Wow. You look awful."

"Nicky!" Janie scolded.

But Caitlin laughed. "I do, don't I?"

Chase stepped close. "She looks beautiful to me."

"So it's true." Jazzy rolled her eyes. "Love really is blind."

Caitlin's cheeks warmed as she gave Chase a shy smile. They hadn't had time to talk alone since leaving the cabin last night. First the ambulance had whisked her off to the hospital, and then she'd been surrounded by doctors and police officers. Then Jazzy and Liz had shown up after seeing the AMBER Alert on television. They'd been even more hysterical than Caitlin.

As the group headed for the exit, Caitlin tugged on Chase's hand and they fell in step behind the others. "I haven't properly thanked you for coming to rescue me."

"Don't thank me. It was my fault you got tangled up with Alex to begin with." A soft sigh deflated his shoulders. "I am so sorry, Caitlin. I never meant to put you in danger."

Caitlin stopped in the aisle and faced him. She couldn't believe her ears. "What are you talking about? None of this was your fault."

"I worked with him for a year and never saw what he really was. And then I gave you that candle. If I hadn't—"

She stopped his words by placing her fingers gently against his lips. "Don't ever regret your acts of kindness, Chase."

Emotion glowed in his eyes as he brought his hand up to cover hers. "I heard what you said to Alex. Right at the end, I was outside the window, trying to decide how to get in." He shook his head slowly. "I've never known anyone who would spend their last breath trying to convince their killer that God loves them."

"You don't know how you'll act until you're in that situation. You might do exactly the same thing." She gave an embarrassed laugh. "Not that I was all that persuasive."

He put a finger beneath her chin and gently raised her face. "You never know. He's going to have a long time to think about what you told him. God might use your words yet."

Chase was right. She closed her eyes. *Lord, don't let Alex forget. Remind him of Your love every day.*

She opened her eyes to find Chase's face inches from hers. Had he leaned close to her, or had she moved toward him? Either way, he was close enough for her to feel his warm breath on her cheek.

With a sharp pang of regret, she backed away from him. "We're about to violate the dateless year."

He heaved a regretful sigh. "So, you're still determined to continue that, huh?"

Caitlin bit her lip. She'd spent much of last night struggling with that question, and she didn't like the conclusion she'd come to.

"I have to, Chase. Please understand." She placed a hand on his arm. "I love you. I'm certain of it. But I made a commitment, and I don't take that lightly."

A slow smile curved his mouth. "You know, when I left you and your friends at the hotel last night, I had a long talk with my cousin. He's planning a trip to Florida to meet a woman he's been corresponding with through e-mail. He's never met this woman, and he's starting to sound like he thinks she's the one for him. It made me realize that we don't have to live in the same town to get to know each other." He grabbed her hand and squeezed. "We can be long-distance…friends. It really could work, if we try hard." He grinned. "At least for a year."

"Not even a full year. Three hundred sixty-three and a half days." Caitlin couldn't hold back her own grin. "But who's counting?"

He leaned close. For a breathless moment, she thought he

might kiss her, but instead, his lips brushed her ear with a whisper. "I am."

Joy settled in Caitlin's heart as she looked into Chase's eyes. She'd come to Little Nashville devastated over a broken romance and the loss of her best friends. But God had given her a precious new friend—and one day, he would become much more. A giggle broke free as she left the church, hand in hand with her favorite candle maker.

EPILOGUE

Three hundred sixty-three and a half days later

Caitlin turned in front of the mirror. The silky red fabric of her skirt fluttered below her knees. A flush rode high on her cheeks, and the color set off a sparkle in her blue eyes.

She whirled toward Jazzy, who lay propped on pillows against her headboard, Sassy snuggled close to her side. Her friend had made the four-hour trip from Waynesboro to be with Caitlin on this oh-so-important day. "What do you think?"

Jazzy's hand rested on her pregnant belly. "You look incredible."

"No fair!" Liz's voice projected from the speaker phone on the night stand. "I want to see. Jazzy, take a picture and send it to me."

"Okay, hold on a minute."

Caitlin struck a pose while Jazzy snapped a picture with her cell phone, and then returned to the mirror to brush a tiny bit more mascara on her eyelashes. The moment the photo arrived on Liz's phone in Utah, she heard a gasp through the speaker.

"Cate, you're stunning! Chase won't be able to take his eyes off of you."

Jazzy snorted. "After making the guy wait a full year for your first date, you could be wearing a potato sack and he'd fall at your feet."

"I have to admit, I didn't think you'd make it." Liz's voice held a grudging respect. "I figured he'd get tired of waiting and find someone else."

Caitlin gave the dress a final whirl, then sank onto the mattress beside Jazzy. "I worried about that at first," she confessed, "but I shouldn't have. We've grown close." Her cheeks warmed. "We didn't have to go out on dates to fall in love. I think we've gotten to know each other better than some couples ever do. We've e-mailed a dozen times every day, and talked to each other every night on the phone. And we have spent some time together, just as friends. It hasn't been easy, but we made it." She giggled. "I think it's been harder on Chase's mom than anyone else."

"Well, she's got to be happy that you're moving to Indiana," Liz said.

"Are you sure you want to do that?" Jazzy asked. "Your life is here. Your parents, your students. Everything."

"It's only a few hours' drive." Caitlin patted the hand on her belly. "Mom and Dad are fine with it. And Little Nashville is an artist colony. What better place for a flute teacher? I already have one student. I'll get more."

The memory of Nicky's excitement when Caitlin told her she was moving to town brought a smile to Caitlin's face. The girl had already started spreading the word among her friends that "the world's most awesome flute teacher is coming *here!*"

Jazzy glanced out the window, then leaped to her feet. She held the curtain back and turned a grin Caitlin's way. "Come look at this."

Caitlin looked through the window. A shiny black limousine was parked outside her apartment building. She brought a hand up to cover her mouth. "Oh, my."

"What? What is it?" Liz's voice demanded.

"This guy is pulling out all the stops tonight," Jazzy told her. "He just arrived in a limo."

The doorbell rang. Sassy leaped off the bed, yapping, and raced from the room. The flutter of a dozen hummingbird wings erupted behind Caitlin's ribcage. "He's here!"

As she ran out of the bedroom, she heard Liz's voice issue a command from the speaker. "Jazzy, get pictures."

Caitlin rushed to the door.

"Slow down," Jazzy hissed. "It's totally uncool to look like you're in a hurry."

But Caitlin had waited long enough for this night. No more waiting. She threw the door open wide.

Chase stood outside, his warm smile betraying a hint of the eagerness that pounded in her chest. Her breath caught in her throat. Some part of her brain registered his black tux, his hair the color of ripened wheat, the bouquet of red roses in his hand. But it was his eyes that held hers captive.

He opened his arms, and without a second thought, Caitlin stepped into them. As she raised her arms to circle his neck, she heard the click of Jazzy's camera phone behind her. A giggle erupted from her throat. Oh, what an incredible feeling, to be held in Chase's embrace. Her heart thundered, and she wanted never to move—ever.

Chase's warm breath caressed her cheek as he whispered, "Hello, my friend."

In the next instant, his lips touched hers. The dateless year had come to a perfect end. The world fell away as Caitlin surrendered to the kiss of her best friend.

* * * * *

Dear Reader,

The idea for SCENT OF MURDER came to me as a candle flickered on the corner of my desk and filled my office with the scent of cinnamon. Of course, I've never actually made a candle. I naively thought I'd just place a few phone calls, take a tour and learn everything I needed to know. I soon discovered that candle makers guard their secrets as jealously as my grandmother guarded her fried chicken recipe. Thank goodness I finally found Janet Stephens, who didn't mind sharing her expertise with me. If you're ever in Bowling Green, Kentucky, I encourage you to visit Candle Makers on the Square and check out the awesome scents they offer. (Don't miss my favorite—Cinnamon Red Hots!)

I've spent many hours in Little Nashville, a town nestled in the beautiful Blue Hills of Indiana. The quaint village-like feel of the shopping area I've portrayed in SCENT OF MURDER is real. Everything else is fictitious, including Ed Graham's candle shop and Chase's factory. That's the best part of being a writer—I can rearrange entire towns to suit my purposes.

Thank you for reading SCENT OF MURDER. I hope you'll let me know what you thought of my book. Please take a moment to contact me through my Web site—www.Virginia-Smith.org.

Virginia Smith

QUESTIONS FOR DISCUSSION

1. Some people avoid reminders of unpleasant memories, but Chase is unable to stay away from the area in the park where his friend was killed. Why does that place haunt him?

2. What prompts Caitlin to make the decision for a dateless year? Is this a wise decision?

3. Caitlin struggles with conflicting emotions regarding her friends' upcoming weddings. What interferes with her being completely happy for them?

4. When does Caitlin first realize she has feelings for Chase? Is she "on the rebound," as she fears?

5. What is your favorite flavor of ice cream, and what might that say about your personality?

6. Chase describes Caitlin as "a nurturer." Identify ways she exhibits this quality throughout the book.

7. Caitlin and Chase both experience unexpected feelings of compassion or concern for people who don't deserve them. Identify those instances, and discuss why these feelings may have occurred.

8. Caitlin prays repeatedly for someone to see her and Nicky when they are being abducted. How is her prayer answered? Have you had times when your prayers seem to go unanswered?

9. Maude tells Chase and Detective Jenkins that she knew Caitlin was upset because "the Lord stirred my soul." Does that really happen? Discuss a time you may have felt your soul stirred.

10. The Scripture theme for this book is, "Blesssed are the merciful, for they shall be shown mercy." (Matthew 5:7, NIV) In what ways is that verse illustrated in *Scent of Murder?*

11. Are there benefits in developing a friendship before entering into a romantic relationship with someone you're attracted to?

12. If you read the first two books in this series, *A Taste of Murder* and *Murder at Eagle Summit,* which character did you most identify with—Jazzy, Liz or Caitlin?

When a tornado strikes a small Kansas town, Maya Logan sees a new, tender side of her serious boss. Could a family man be lurking beneath Greg Garrison's gruff exterior?

Turn the page for a sneak preview of their story in
HEALING THE BOSS'S HEART
by Valerie Hansen,
Book 1 in the new six-book
AFTER THE STORM miniseries
available beginning July 2009 from Love Inspired®.

Maya Logan had been watching the skies with growing concern and already had her car keys in hand when she jerked open the door to the office to admit her boss. He held a young boy in his arms. "Get inside. Quick!"

Gregory Garrison thrust the squirming child at her. "Here. Take him. I'm going back after his dog. He refused to come in out of the storm without Charlie."

"Don't be ridiculous." She clutched his arm and pointed. "You'll never catch him. Look." Tommy's dog had taken off running the minute the hail had started.

Debris was swirling through the air in ever-increasing amounts and the hail had begun to pile in lumpy drifts along the curb. It had flattened the flowers she'd so lovingly placed in the planters and buried their stubbly remnants under inches of white, icy crystals.

In the distance, the dog had its tail between its legs and was disappearing into the maelstrom. Unless the frightened animal responded to commands to return, there was no chance of anyone catching up to it.

Gregory took a deep breath and hollered, "Char-lie," but

Maya could tell he was wasting his breath. The soggy mongrel didn't even slow.

"Take the boy and head for the basement," Gregory yelled at her. Ducking inside, he had to put his shoulder to the heavy door and use his full weight to close and latch it.

She shoved Tommy back at him. "No. I have to go get Layla."

"In this weather? Don't be an idiot."

"She's my daughter. She's only three. She'll be scared to death if I'm not there."

"She's in the preschool at the church, right? They'll take care of the kids."

"No. I'm going after her."

"Use your head. You can't help Layla if you get yourself killed." He grasped her wrist, holding tight.

Maya struggled, twisting her arm till it hurt. "Let me go. I'm going to my baby. She's all I've got."

"That's crazy! A tornado is coming. If the hail doesn't knock you out cold, the tornado's likely to bury you."

"I don't care."

"Yes, you do."

"No, I don't! Let go of me." To her amazement, he held fast. No one, especially a man, was going to treat her this way and get away with it. No one.

"Stop. Think," he shouted, staring at her as if she were deranged.

She continued to struggle, to refuse to give in to his will, his greater strength. "No. *You* think. I'm going to my little girl. That's all there is to it."

"How? Driving?" He indicated the street, which now looked distorted due to the vibrations of the front window. "It's too late. Look at those cars. Your head isn't half as hard as that metal is and it's already full of dents."

"But…"

She knew in her mind that he was right, yet her heart kept insisting she must do something. Anything. *Please, God, help me. Tell me what to do!*

Her heart was still pounding, her breath shallow and rapid, yet part of her seemed to suddenly accept that her boss was right. That couldn't be. She belonged with Layla. She was her mother.

"We're going to take shelter," Gregory ordered, giving her arm a tug. "Now."

That strong command was enough to renew Maya's resolve and wipe away the calm assurances she had so briefly embraced. She didn't go easily or quietly. Screeching, "No, no, no," she dragged her feet, stumbling along as he pulled and half dragged her toward the basement access.

Staring into the storm moments ago, she had felt as if the fury of the weather was sucking her into a bottomless black hole. Her emotions were still trapped in those murky, imaginary depths, still floundering, sinking, spinning out of control. She pictured Layla, with her silky, long dark hair and beautiful brown eyes.

"If anything happens to my daughter I'll never forgive you!" she screamed at him.

"I'll take my chances."

Maya knew without a doubt that she'd meant exactly what she'd said. If her precious little girl was hurt she'd never forgive herself for not trying to reach her. To protect her. And she'd never forgive Gregory Garrison for preventing her from making the attempt. *Never.*

She had to blink to adjust to the dimness of the basement as he shoved her in front of him and forced her down the wooden stairs.

She gasped, coughed. The place smelled musty and sour, totally in character with the advanced age of the building. How long could that bank of brick and stone stores and offices stand against a storm like this? If these walls ever started to topple, nothing would stop their total collapse. Then it wouldn't matter whether they were outside or down here. They'd be just as dead.

That realization sapped her strength and left her almost without sensation. When her boss let go of her wrist and slipped his arm around her shoulders to guide her into a corner next to an abandoned elevator shaft, she was too emotionally numb to continue to fight him. All she could do was pray and continue to repeat, "Layla, Layla," over and over again.

"We'll wait it out here," he said. "This has to be the strongest part of the building."

Maya didn't believe a word he said.

Tommy's quiet sobbing, coupled with her soul-deep concern for her little girl, brought tears to her eyes. She blinked them back, hoping she could control her emotions enough to fool the boy into believing they were all going to come through the tornado unhurt.

As for her, she wasn't sure. Not even the tiniest bit.

All she could think about was her daughter. *Dear Lord, are You watching out for Layla? Please, please, please! Take care of my precious little girl.*

* * * * *

See the rest of Maya and Greg's story when
HEALING THE BOSS'S HEART
hits the shelves in July 2009.
And be sure to look for all six of the books in the
AFTER THE STORM series, where you can follow
the residents of High Plains, Kansas,
as they rebuild their town—and find love in the process.

HEARTWARMING INSPIRATIONAL ROMANCE

Experience stories
centered on love and faith
with a variety of romances
just for you,
with 10 books every month!

Love Inspired®:
Enjoy four contemporary,
heartwarming romances every month.

Love Inspired® *Historical:*
Travel to a different time with two powerful
and engaging stories of romance, adventure
and faith every month.

Love Inspired® *Suspense:*
Enjoy four contemporary tales of intrigue
and romance every month.

Steeple Hill®

*Available every month wherever books are
sold, including most bookstores, supermarkets,
drugstores and discount stores.*

REQUEST YOUR FREE BOOKS!
2 FREE RIVETING INSPIRATIONAL NOVELS
PLUS 2 FREE MYSTERY GIFTS

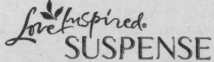

Love Inspired®
SUSPENSE

YES! Please send me 2 FREE Love Inspired® Suspense novels and my 2 FREE mystery gifts (gifts are worth about $10). After receiving them, if I don't wish to receive any more books, I can return the shipping statement marked "cancel". If I don't cancel, I will receive 4 brand-new novels every month and be billed just $4.24 per book in the U.S. or $4.74 per book in Canada. That's a savings of over 20% off the cover price. It's quite a bargain! Shipping and handling is just 50¢ per book.* I understand that accepting the 2 free books and gifts places me under no obligation to buy anything. I can always return a shipment and cancel at any time. Even if I never buy another book, the two free books and gifts are mine to keep forever.

123 IDN EYM2   323 IDN EYNE

Name	(PLEASE PRINT)	
Address		Apt. #
City	State/Prov.	Zip/Postal Code

Signature (if under 18, a parent or guardian must sign)

Mail to Steeple Hill Reader Service:
IN U.S.A.: P.O. Box 1867, Buffalo, NY 14240-1867
IN CANADA: P.O. Box 609, Fort Erie, Ontario L2A 5X3

Not valid to current subscribers of Love Inspired Suspense books.

Want to try two free books from another series?
Call 1-800-873-8635 or visit www.morefreebooks.com

* Terms and prices subject to change without notice. Prices do not include applicable taxes. Sales tax applicable in N.Y. Canadian residents will be charged applicable provincial taxes and GST. Offer not valid in Quebec. This offer is limited to one order per household. All orders subject to approval. Credit or debit balances in a customer's account(s) may be offset by any other outstanding balance owed by or to the customer. Please allow 4 to 6 weeks for delivery. Offer available while quantities last.

Your Privacy: Steeple Hill Books is committed to protecting your privacy. Our Privacy Policy is available online at www.SteepleHill.com or upon request from the Reader Service. From time to time we make our lists of customers available to reputable third parties who may have a product or service of interest to you. If you would prefer we not share your name and address, please check here. ☐

Love Inspired
SUSPENSE

TITLES AVAILABLE NEXT MONTH

Available July 14, 2009

WITNESS TO MURDER by Jill Elizabeth Nelson

Poised for an interview, TV reporter Hallie Berglund walks into a murder scene instead. She wants the killer brought to justice—but has she identified the right man? Her colleague Brody Jordan knows Hallie can find the truth...if she's willing to unearth the secrets of the past.

SOMEONE TO TRUST by Ginny Aiken

Carolina Justice

So what if she's the fire chief's daughter? Arson investigator Rand Mason knows too much about Catelyn Caldwell's past to trust her. Yet Cate's not the girl he remembers. And when she needs Rand's help, it's time to see if she's become someone he can believe in—and love.

DEADLY INTENT by Camy Tang

The Grant family's Sonoma spa is a place for rest and relaxation—not murder! Then Naomi Grant finds her client bleeding to death, and everything falls apart. Naomi's reputation and freedom are at stake, and her only solace is with the *other* suspect, Dr. Devon Knightley, the victim's ex-husband. But he's hiding something from Naomi....

THE KIDNAPPING OF KENZIE THORN by Liz Johnson

Myles Parsons is just another inmate in Kenzie Thorn's GED course—until he kidnaps her and reveals the truth. He's Myles Borden, FBI agent, undercover because someone wants her dead. But he promises he'll keep her safe. His heart won't accept anything else.

LISCNMBPA0609